Whiskey, Guns & Cows

Whiskey, Guns & Cows

James A. Lawrence

James A. Lawrence

Copyright ©1992 by James A. Lawrence
Dust jacket painting copyright ©1992 by Lisa Harvey

All rights reserved, including the right to reproduce this book or parts thereof, except for the inclusion of brief quotations in a review.

Library of Congress Catalog Card Number: 92-74572
ISBN: 1-56044-182-8

Published by Lawrence Publishing
P.O. Box 272
Newport, Washington 99156
in cooperation with SkyHouse Publishers, an imprint of Falcon Press Publishing Co., Inc., Helena, Montana.

Design, typesetting, and other prepress work by Falcon Graphics, Helena, Montana

Distributed by Falcon Press Publishing Co., Inc.
P.O. Box 1718, Helena, Montana 59624, or call 1-800-582-2665.

First Edition

Manufactured in the United States of America

*To Dorothy
and her undying faith*

one

The glass shattered against the hitching rail. A tall, rangy cowboy with watery blue eyes held the broken bottle to Will Bowman's trembling throat. "I don't give a damn if you are the sheriff. Nobody tells me how much to drink! I can hold my liquor better'n any man alive, and don't you forget..." The bottle slipped from his hand as he stared in amazement at the rising sun. Muttering to himself, he turned and staggered down the boardwalk.

Sheriff Bowman wiped the perspiration from his forehead. Nervously, he looked around. No one else was on the street. Suddenly his fear turned to anger. Delmar was not worth the jail space he took up. Something would have to be done.

The town of Crooked Fork, Texas, sprawled in herringbone fashion, like a drunken sailor trying to walk a floating wharf in a high wind. The false fronts of antiquated stores facing the crooked street called Main were five years overdue for a paint job. The gray, discolored boards just sat, soaking up the sun. Neglected boardwalks groaned, and even the hitching rails sagged in the middle, warped from years in the sun and rain. The store owners were either too lazy or just refused to give a damn. Maybe it was too much work or too little money, but somewhere along the way they had lost their pride.

Crooked Fork began as a stage stop and, as it grew, cow ranches sprang up here and there. The merchants built to suit themselves with no thought for the future, and as years passed it became a joke. The townspeople claimed only a drunk could ride straight out of town in any direction.

A stranger riding into town could swear it was an election year. Posters hung on every building and fence post for twenty miles in all directions. The message to ranchers read: *Meeting to be held March 2, at the courthouse at seven o'clock. Bring your foremen. Trail drive to Kansas, Wichita, or Dodge. This drive needs an experienced trail boss. Thompson Brothers Cattle Company.*

It was known far and wide that the ranchers around Crooked Fork had tried for three years to put a trail drive together. They had failed miserably. But this time was different. Once and for all, the ranchers agreed. The range was running low on grass, and the only way to cure the problem was to reduce the size of the herds. Added to that, the local bank could carry no more debt. The choice became evident: make the drive or go broke. The talk was fourteen dollars a head in Kansas. That kind of money would put most of the ranchers back in the black ink and definitely make the bankers happy.

The weather was cool and the ranchers were in good spirits. The family men brought their wives along, figuring the womenfolk could do their spring shopping. Some lived a considerable distance from town, so why not combine business and pleasure? On any other given business day, the town of Crooked Fork looked deserted except for a few drummers selling their wares and an occasional drifter. Saturday afternoon and night were different. The local cowboys lined up at the bars and cafes, and the hotel was full.

That day, the town began to fill up early. The meeting was to start at seven o'clock sharp at the courthouse, the biggest building in town. Somehow, by accident, the courthouse sat square in the center of town. One had to drive around it to get from one side of town to the other. By six-thirty, the courtroom was filled to capacity, standing room only. Everyone was on his best behavior; ranch hands had been warned against fighting in saloons or anywhere else.

Horses, surreys, and wagons lined the streets. Children and dogs ran freely up and down the boardwalks, the dogs barking with excitement. The men gathered at the courthouse and the women were left to do their spring shopping while keeping a watchful eye on the children.

The prudish local sheriff and his deputy tried their best to make everyone feel at ease, talking to one person then another, especially solicitous due to the election coming up in the fall.

Ned Thompson of the Thompson Cattle Company rubbed his long jaw with his knobby knuckles as he picked up the gavel and hammered the crowd to silence. After a moment or two, Ned began, his deep booming voice filling the room. "You all know why we're gathered here. We have to get our beef to market. Any of you who have beef to join a trail drive, put your name and head of cattle on the paper the sheriff has given you. Only the ones with cattle to ship will be qualified to vote on the other business."

Unnerved, Ned slumped into his seat. That short speech was the most he had spoken in a whole year. Ben Thompson, two years younger, was not blessed with the gift of gab either. Socializing was not something they did.

Taking care not to hurt his good-old-boy image, Sheriff Will Bowman gingerly escorted the curious onlookers out. His careful handling took almost an hour, and the cattlemen were becoming impatient. Finally, Ben Thompson wielded the gavel, and the count was taken. Some twenty-three signatures were collected with approximately seven thousand head of cattle consigned to the drive. Ben read the numbers aloud. The next order of business was election of a trail boss. Everyone knew the rules: the one chosen must know the trail.

After a long silence, Ned spoke. "I don't think anyone here knows the trail, let alone how to drive a cow up Kansas way." After another long pause, he growled, "Well, damn it, speak up somebody! We got thousands of cows, plenty of men, and no boss." The room was quiet.

Everyone present realized that such a large herd would get a lot of attention. Every lowlife gunslinger, road agent, and outlaw would be watching. And that did not include Cheyennes, Arapahoes, half-breeds, and God knows what else.

Ned spoke again. "We want the best trail boss we can get. I think I speak for everyone here." The crowd murmured in agreement. "Well, who's the best, any of you know? You all talk it over a mite."

The room buzzed with conversation while the Thompson brothers sat on the judge's bench.

After twenty minutes, Ben Thompson addressed the crowd. "Okay now," he began, "have we got a man to vote on?"

John Roper stood and answered. "Yes, Ben, we got one."

"Well, John, tell us so we can get this over with."

"It's Delmar." John Roper spoke the name softly, a note of concern in his voice.

"You mean Dry Bottle Delmar?"

The crowd began to laugh as Ben stood smiling.

"One and the same," John Roper answered.

"He ain't nothin' but the town drunk. You must of took leave of your good sense, John," Ben said.

"What you say is true," John admitted. "But he's the man that's goin' to drive my cows."

A hush fell over the courtroom. All eyes were on John Roper. Ben Thompson found his voice again and his smile disappeared. He knew that John Roper was serious.

"He hasn't drawn a sober breath since I knowed him," Ben muttered.

Ned agreed. "He ain't seen the sun through clear eyes in years. I bet he thinks the sun is deep red."

The crowd started to laugh again.

"What makes you think he can do the job, John?" Ben Thompson asked.

John Roper's answer came slowly. "Gentlemen, I know him. We all know him. I don't think there's a man here who hasn't bought him a bottle one time or another. Have any of you ever asked yourselves what he did before he came here?"

The crowd grew quiet again. After all, John Roper was the second largest cattle owner around Crooked Fork. He must have his reasons.

"I happen to know who and what he was. I brought him here in the first place and I'm guilty of buying most of his booze. Crazy Bill Anderson and I rode with Dry Bottle Delmar in the war. There's no better man with a gun or a knife. Just ask Crazy Bill how he got his limp. Gentlemen, Delmar is the reason I stand before you tonight—he saved my life more than once. I will personally stand behind him."

John Roper stood straight and tall. "I might add, gentlemen, he knows Kansas like the palm of his hand. He was born there."

"John, we all know you to be a man of your word. But damn it, John, it would take a month to dry him out. No offense meant," Ned said. "And another thing, if he is as good as you say, then why don't he work for you now?"

John Roper looked at the waiting crowd. He was prepared for the question.

"He won't work for nobody but himself. Claims if he has a boss to answer to he can't be himself. And every officer I knew in the war said the same thing, that Major Delmar was not to be led, he was the leader. Would any of you work for someone else if your family was killed and your ranch taken away? You've all heard about the carpetbaggers. I repeat, my cattle go with Delmar or they don't go at all. Drunk or no drunk," John Roper whispered to himself as he sat down.

▲▲▲

two

As Roper sat down, Bill Downs, his foreman, nodded in agreement. Everyone in the room knew Bill Downs. He worked like hell, played the same way, and fought at the drop of a hat. He had been Roper's foreman as long as anyone cared to remember, the kind of foreman every rancher prayed for but seldom got. After an hour and a half of bickering and yelling, it was Bill Downs who finally convinced them that Dry Bottle Delmar was the man for the job. According to Bill, not only was Delmar the best man with horses he had ever seen, he damn sure knew cows.

"We know we can trust you, Bill. But damn it, man, it completely blows us over for the town drunk to be trail boss," a big, chesty rancher shouted.

Bill smiled. "I know," he admitted, "but let me tell you something, Mr. Covington. Dry Bottle Delmar is one hell of a man. Crazy Bill Anderson claimed Delmar could shoot the wings off a hummingbird and not disturb its sex life."

Laughter rippled through the crowd, relieving the tension in the room.

A vote was taken, not that it made much difference. John Roper had already made his decision, and without John's vote on anything, it would fail. Ben Thompson banged his gavel and read the outcome: nineteen for Delmar, four against. But the majority agreed with Roper on one condition, that Bill Downs accompany Delmar. Roper's argument that he needed Bill on the ranch was quickly met with every kind of opposition.

The crowd would not accept Delmar alone. Without Bill there was no trail drive. Roper finally agreed. Bill Downs would be the ramrod, Dry Bottle Delmar the trail boss.

The meeting broke up, and as the new ramrod pushed through the crowd, Nellie Howard and her sister Teresa attracted his attention. The sisters owned a good-sized ranch, commonly known as "the widow-women place" since Jess Howard had been killed. Nellie would not give up the ranch. Her sister Teresa, also a widow, had come to live with her. Although he knew them by sight, Bill was not well acquainted with either one. Both smiled as Bill approached with a question in his eyes.

"We both want you to know, Mr. Downs, that we have confidence in you. We're sending a thousand head on the drive."

"Well, thank you, ladies." Bill quickly came to the conclusion that they were very handsome women. It was easy to tell that they were sisters. Although Nellie was some ten pounds heavier than Teresa, they both had dark hair, dark eyes, and well-developed figures. Their enthusiastic greetings and the sparkle in their eyes made Bill's pulse rise a few beats.

"We sure will be glad to get our beef to market," Teresa said. "It's been a long time since we've seen any real money."

"I believe everyone shares your sentiments," Bill replied slowly.

"I understand some of the banks are loaned dry," Nellie said.

Bill nodded. "Yes ma'am, I believe you're right. If you ladies will excuse me..."

"Oh, one more thing, Mr. Downs," Teresa burst out. "I'm sure one of us is going with you."

Bill was struck dumb. When he finally found his voice, he said, "You're kidding me!"

"No. One of us is going, right Nellie?"

"Yes, of course. Where our cattle are concerned, we intend to be well-represented."

As the color drained from his face, Bill swallowed hard and said, "There'll be plenty of men to do the job, I'm sure. No use for a couple of beauties like you to put yourselves in danger with a cattle drive."

"Your flattery sounds good, Mr. Downs, but like I said, we'll represent ourselves."

▲▲▲

three

It took two days for word to reach surrounding towns. Some of the bankers, nervous about risking their money on a cattle drive led by Dry Bottle Delmar, urged the ranchers to drop out. A thousand-mile cattle drive was dangerous enough, but led by the town drunk? Never! Surely no one could be serious about such an insane plan.

The townspeople of Crooked Fork decided to buy Delmar another drink and everything would be forgotten. To their surprise, Dry Bottle Delmar had already gotten drunk and passed out.

The day of the meeting, as he watched the people gathering, Delmar's 180-pound, six-foot frame swayed like a leaf in a gentle wind. In his whiskey-fogged brain, he pondered the cause of all the commotion. It was the most people he had seen in over a year. Maybe the war had started all over again.

"I sure hope not," Delmar mumbled to himself. "I don't want to fight anymore."

The memories of his past flooded back into his besotted brain. Chickamauga was where he had seen all the dead men, or was it Horse

Head Ridge? Delmar shook his head. "Damned if I know. Maybe I died and this is hell I'm wandering around in."

One thing he did know: his throat was dry and he needed another drink. He staggered toward Crooked Fork Bar, bumping into the hitching rail. He stopped and stared. "Damn! Since when did they build a fence across the boardwalk?" He found himself nose to nose with a horse. "You need a drink, too?" he asked as he put out his hand to pat the horse's neck.

"Don't breathe on my horse, Dry Bottle. I can't ride him drunk! Come on, I'll help you over to the bar." A strong hand turned him around.

"Hello, Tim. What're you doin' in town?"

Tim Hubberd replied indulgently, "Come on, Delmar. You better get off the street or you'll wind up in jail again."

Tim Hubberd had worked for John Roper for three years and understood his feelings toward Delmar. He had been told not to abuse him, to help him whenever he could. After bumping their way through the door, they finally made their way into the bar.

"I ain't goin' to say thanks," Delmar muttered. "I didn't ask you to, did I?"

Tim sat him in a chair at the end of the bar, where he would be out of the way. *Damn ungrateful bastard,* Tim thought to himself. As he left, Delmar sat starry-eyed, comprehending nothing. Slumping further down in the chair, he crossed his arms on the bar, put his head down, and passed out. No one paid any attention to him; he was just the town drunk.

The bar was full, but most patrons kept their voices low. The cowboys had been given fair warning not to cause trouble. Each and every one knew it could mean his job if he got out of line. The fat, bald bartender cast a watchful eye toward Delmar throughout the afternoon, but it was close to six o'clock before Delmar raised his head to gaze around the room. His throat felt like cotton, his belly was on fire, and his hands shook. He needed a drink, and bad.

The bartender quickly poured a drink and passed it to him. "Here you go. This is on Roper."

Delmar downed the drink in one gulp, allowing a few drops to dribble down his unshaven chin. He slowly wiped it off with the back of his hand.

"You better get some air," the bartender suggested. "Come back after a while." It was his way of saying *no more whiskey for now.* Delmar sheepishly picked his hat up off the floor and stumbled from the barroom. "Too damn noisy in here, anyhow," he rasped.

The sun was setting, he noticed, as he went outside. He put his hands up to his face. God, how his head hurt. As he leaned up against the wall trying to put the pieces together, Bill Downs appeared from out of nowhere.

"John wants you to come to the meeting over at the courthouse. Best we get started in that direction."

Delmar turned and followed Bill through the crowded street. "What does John want with me?" he mumbled.

"I don't know," Bill replied over his shoulder. "All I know is he said to bring you."

Confused, Delmar wandered into the courtroom after Bill. But as Bill and John Roper tried to convince the ranchers to choose Dry Bottle Delmar, their would-be trail boss slipped out the door and was gone.

In his drunken stupor, Delmar somehow got the idea that he was the cause of all the trouble. It appeared that his old friend John Roper had helped him. Otherwise he would be in jail. He was no stranger to the town jail. He could not remember how many days and nights he had spent there, nor did he care.

Exhausted, he tried the door to the local whorehouse. Winney, the madam, told him to get lost. "I'm not buyin' another damn drink for you!" she shouted after him.

Whiskey, Guns & Cows

Only one other place to go. Delmar hobbled toward the back of the hotel and his Chinaman friend. The Chinaman would let him sleep in the hall to the kitchen, just outside his room. More than anything, Delmar needed sleep. He still had half a pint in his hip pocket, a hideout bottle, just in case. He kept it under his shirt in his belt. As lightning flashed across the sky, he slipped in the back door of the hotel. He sat down in the hallway, took a long pull on his bottle and curled up like a dog on the floor.

The Chinaman cook at the hotel, known only as Sing, was working late. Coming through the hallway, he found Delmar curled up beside his hat on the floor. Both hands full, Sing stopped and sat the buckets on the floor. He did not want to step on Delmar or his hat, so he carefully picked up the hat, and for want of a better place, put it on his head. Besides, it was raining. Sing picked up his buckets and went out.

"I must be dreaming," Sing said to himself. There was no way he could be tied across a saddle on his belly. He was soaked with rain and his head hurt. Only his pride kept him from crying out in pain. He was sure he had eaten his last bowl of rice or anything else. He was surely going to die. He prayed silently that someone who knew him would ship his body back to the motherland.

When he opened his almond-shaped eyes again, he was standing with the help of two cowboys. It was daylight, and an angry John Roper stood before him. He was cussing everybody he could think of. "You guys are the dumbest bunch of cow jockeys I've ever seen. Can't you tell the difference between a pigtailed Chinaman and the town drunk? Now you take him back."

Weak as he was, Sing had no intention of going back the way he came out. He tried to jerk free so he could run.

"Are you all right?" John Roper kept asking him.

Sing spoke little English, and after being hit on the head, all he could remember was, "Gee Klist, boss. Gee Klist."

"Turn him loose," Roper ordered.

The cowboys let go and Sing slipped to the ground, holding his head. Roper could see a good-sized knot on his head and again asked him how he was.

"Gee Klist, boss. Gee Klist," Sing mumbled.

"Get the surrey over here. Bill, take him to a doctor."

Still holding his head, Sing sat up. Roper wanted to help the Chinaman, but all he could get out of him was "Gee Klist, boss," which made no sense at all.

Roper watched the men hustle around to get the surrey. The rain had stopped and water stood in small pools everywhere. The team came up at a trot to where Roper stood, spraying mud and water all over him and the Chinaman.

Sing repeated, "Gee Klist, boss. Gee Klist."

Roper agreed. "Gee Klist! Watch where you're going," he yelled. He suddenly realized he was echoing the Chinaman.

"You learnin' to speak Chinese?" Bill Downs asked.

"Shut up, Bill. Don't say a damn word and put your shirttail in. You look like hell."

All at once it struck Bill what had happened, and he sat right down in the mud, laughing until his sides hurt.

"Laugh, you jackass!" Roper yelled. "Help me get this Chink loaded and back to town."

"Gee Klist, boss, I can't get up." Bill laughed some more, then struggled to his feet, wiped the tears from his eyes, and helped load the Chinaman.

"Who brained this Chink anyway?" Bill asked.

"I did," Shorty Driedon answered. "And it ain't funny, Bill."

"Can't you tell the difference between Dry Bottle and a Chink?" Bill asked.

"Hell yes, I can, but he come out the back door of the hotel wearin' Dry Bottle's hat and it bein' dark and all.... Besides, we had us a little touch over at the Bull's Head waitin' 'til it got dark."

"Touch, my ass! You must of took a bath in it. I swear you've been drinkin' Old Bone Breaker and it all went to your head. You can't tell a Chink from a drunk. Never mind, Shorty, but Gee Klist the boss is mad. Now go get Dry Bottle and don't come out here with anything else."

When John Roper overheard Bill talking to Shorty, one of his oldest and most dependable men, he knew it was an honest mistake.

He walked to the surrey and said, "Shorty, you take this Chink in to the doctor. Stay in town and get some sleep today. But tonight, Bill and some more of our crew will help get Dry Bottle out here, won't you Bill?"

Bill burst out laughing again. "Yeah, boss, I will, but Gee Klist, it'll be a long time before you live this down."

Roper grinned. "You're probably right." He turned and walked back to the ranch house.

▲▲▲

four

Two days later Dry Bottle sat shaking in John Roper's bunkhouse. Four nondrinking cowboys had been assigned to watch him day and night.

Besides daily visits from the doctor, they tried every home remedy known to man. If they had it, he swallowed it, from Cayenne pepper to sheep dip.

In spite of their efforts, Delmar sat at the end of a lower bunk, fighting all the wild beasts in the world. His six-foot frame was thin, his eyes sunk deep in their sockets. His whiskers were an inch long, and his face looked like he had passed death by four miles.

John Roper stood watching as they brought Dry Bottle to the main house. He looked like he had just escaped the undertakers.

"Welcome back to our ugly damn world, Delmar," John said with a touch of sympathy.

Delmar nodded as he stepped down from the surrey. "Didn't you think I could walk from the bunkhouse?" he asked.

Roper ignored the remark. "Come on in, we need to talk."

The cowboys left them alone.

"John, this better be good, by God! You bring me out here and try to kill me! God, my guts is sore," Delmar complained.

"To hell with your guts! I probably saved you from pickling what's left of 'em! And furthermore, you once told me if I ever needed you, to tie you to a fence post and dry you out, deep-down depression and excessive misery not included. Well, I need you now."

Delmar sat down, eyeing his oldest and dearest friend. "You're serious, ain't you?" he said.

"Yes, I am. You've been hired to boss a herd north to Kansas."

"Who was so damn stupid as to do that?" Delmar asked.

"Me." Roper offered him a cigar.

"No, not now, John." Delmar stood up and began to pace the floor.

Finally, after half an hour, Roper asked, "Well?"

Delmar stopped and said, "Okay, John, I'll do it, but it'll take me a while to get in shape. And one more thing, if I ever tell you I'll help you again, I want your word you'll shoot me. I wouldn't do this for another damn man in the world."

Roper put out his hand and Delmar accepted. They stood silent for several seconds. Delmar asked, "No one knows, do they, John?"

"No, Delmar, they don't, and as far as I'm concerned they never will." Roper felt sorry for his gaunt, tired friend. "What do you want to do first?"

"Get me a gun and a horse. I won't be much good for a week or so, but with some grub and fresh air...Oh, one more thing, I never want to spend another night as long as I live in that bunkhouse. There's monsters, snakes, and every kind of crawlin' thing known to man in there."

Roper smiled. "Okay, Del, wherever you hang your hat is okay with me. Just so long as you hang it up sober."

Delmar nodded. "It'll be sober, John. In fact, I've drunk my last drop as long as I live. Whoever nicknamed me Dry Bottle won't regret it."

Delmar left the main ranch house, tottering on shaky legs toward the corral.

Ten days had passed since Delmar asked for a horse. Bill Downs had kept a close eye on him. In fact, Bill was beginning to worry. He was sure Delmar was going to walk himself to death. He walked everywhere. Some of the crew even wondered if Delmar intended to round up the cattle on foot.

"Got to build up my legs, you know," he told Bill. "I'll be riding from now on."

"Cut you out a string, Del," Bill said. "We start the spring roundup day after tomorrow."

John Roper watched his crew leave, waving to the driver as the chuck wagon rattled by. He was well-pleased with Delmar's training. Little did anyone know how many miles he and Delmar had walked together. Their old company commander had told them many times, "You can't ride a dead horse. So boys, you're going to learn how to march." And march they did. If the truth were known, they probably walked farther than they rode.

▲▲▲

five

Five weeks later John Roper watched his crew return. The herd stretched for a mile. The cattle were in good shape and the crew had cut out cows over five years old, cows with calves, and yearlings. Roper preferred to ship steers, although he realized that some of the smaller ranchers would ship cows.

After talking far into the night, Roper, Bill Downs, and Dry Bottle Delmar decided to sell two thousand, six hundred head. The next day they worked the cattle for the last time. It was almost dark when the men returned to eat.

Delmar had changed so much. He was clean-shaven, with a quick step and bright eyes, the man Roper remembered.

It was a two-day drive to the rendezvous point, six miles from town. They were the last to arrive. Ned and Ben Thompson met Roper at their campfire, sharing a meal apart from the crew.

"Your herd looks good," Ned remarked.

"Better than some, I suppose," Roper said.

"How many men you sending?" Ben asked.

"Depends on how many we come up with all told." Roper wiped

his mouth on his shirtsleeve as he spoke. "The way we got it figured, we're shipping a few over two thousand, six hundred. You figure three men per thousand?"

"Yeah," Ned grunted. "Sounds good to me."

"I'll tell Delmar. What's our count without mine?"

"So far, five thousand. There were more on paper than that, but some couldn't deliver for one reason or another. So we leave with seven thousand, six hundred head tomorrow. We can't hold them here any longer. That many cows will eat up one hell of a lot of grass."

"What do I tell Delmar is your low dollar?" Roper asked.

"We want at least nine, more if we can get it. We've heard every price from four to twenty-two."

"Okay, Ben, I'll pass the word."

"Can we talk to Bill?" Ned asked.

"Sure, I'll get him over here."

Roper found Delmar and Downs sitting together, drinking coffee. "The Thompson brothers want to talk to you, Bill."

Roper sat down in Bill's place. "They want nine dollars a head for their cattle and I guess ours ain't no better."

Delmar nodded.

"Three men per thousand head sound all right to you?"

"Could use more," Delmar said. "But if it's three men per thousand, I'll need two chuck wagons and extra salt. I'd like a wagonload."

"We'll get it. They'll catch up sometime tomorrow afternoon."

Delmar threw his cold coffee toward the fire. Bill Downs joined them. "We all set, boss?" he asked Delmar.

"Yeah, we leave at first light."

"What did the Thompsons want?" Roper asked.

"Same old shit," Bill said with disgust. "Wanted to know how the drunk was doin'. I told them he worked for me on the roundup, now I work for him. I told them if they wanted to know anything in particular, to ask him. They didn't like what I said, so they left."

"Better get some sleep. Mornin' comes early," Roper said over his shoulder as he walked toward his horse.

The chill of the evening came quickly. After making a last-minute check, Delmar approached Bill Downs. "I'm goin' to town. I'll be back by mornin'. "

Bill started to protest as the thought of Delmar drinking flashed through his mind. *If he gets drunk there won't be no cattle drive—or I'll be boss,* Bill thought to himself. Deep down, Bill knew he did not want and would not take the job. But if Delmar got drunk, it would be interesting to see the outcome. In fact, it would be funny if he did. Bill began to realize that if Delmar got drunk, Roper would have to take the job himself. After all, he had given his word to the ranchers. He was personally responsible, and seven thousand head was a big responsibility no matter who was boss. A voice echoed in Bill's mind, "Gee Klist, boss. Gee Klist." A smile tugged at the corners of his mouth as he watched Delmar ride away.

▲▲▲

six

Delmar rode into Crooked Fork, tying his horse up in front of the hotel. He checked the register. John Roper was registered in room number nine. Delmar went up the stairs and knocked on the door. As the door opened, John stood in his stocking feet, a look of surprise on his face.

"Come in Del. Anything wrong?"

"You're damn right there's something wrong, and you know it! I want some answers to some mighty big questions."

"Like what?"

"Well, to start with, you know and I know there ain't no way in hell that twenty-one men is goin' to drive seven thousand, six hundred head of cattle very damn far. Now how come you went along with them?"

"They outvoted me, Del," John said.

"Well, when I leave here in the mornin', I'm in command, am I not?"

"Yes, you are, Del."

"Well, I want you to send me at least ten more men. Is that understood? And I want at least twenty extra horses and another supply wagon loaded with salt and grub."

"Damn, Del, you didn't have to ride all the way in here to tell me that. I'll be with you for a couple of days."

"I know, John, but you know how I am. If there's something goin' on behind my back, I want to know it."

"I agree with you, Del. I'll get you some more men and I'll have them out there in two or three days."

Del smiled. "Okay, John, I just thought you might know something I didn't. I'll see you tomorrow."

Del closed the door on his way out, then headed back to the herd and his bedroll.

As Bill Downs heard Delmar's horse trot into camp, he thought, *he has to be sober.* Satisfied of that, only then did he allow sleep to overtake him.

Delmar sipped coffee with Bill Downs just before dawn. "I'll take a ride around and see how many ranchers are ready to start," Delmar said coolly. "You start the herd north and the rest will string out behind. Their leaders will mix with our drags and so on. I'll see you about noon." He mounted up and was gone.

Bill rousted out the crew. "Let's get 'em movin', men. Daylight will be here pretty soon."

The cook beat on a frying pan with a metal spoon. "Come and git it before I throw it to the dogs," he yelled. The men took their places in the chow line. Half an hour later they were mounted and moving out.

Delmar stopped at each camp with his tally book. His orders were, "Push 'em north. They'll get strung out today, bunch 'em tonight. Keep all your men for a day or two 'til we get 'em trail broke."

He was welcomed to the small ranchers' camps but got a cold reception from the Thompson brothers. Ned Thompson was waiting when he rode up.

"Where the hell have you been?"

"Doin' my job," Delmar answered. "Why the hell ain't you got these cattle movin' north?"

"That's your job."

"I suggest you take an interest right quick. If you don't help trail break your herd, you'll be standing right here 'til next fall for all I care. And let me say one more thing. If it wasn't for John Roper you could trail your own damn cows. Now get this bunch of so-called cowboys off their asses and move this herd!" Delmar rode away at a gallop, leaving Ned Thompson staring after him.

When Delmar was safely out of earshot, Ned regained his voice, easing his gun in and out of its holster as he spoke. "Why you half-witted drunk! How dare you talk down to me! I'll kill you if you ever speak that way to me again!"

Danny Reed, the Thompson brothers' cow boss, rode up. Seeing the rage in Ned's face, he asked, "Trouble, boss?"

Ned turned quickly. "None of your damn business. Now get this herd movin' north. Stay with it for three days, then come back to the ranch."

Danny looked surprised. He had never seen Ned so angry. He turned quickly and began shouting orders to his men.

Late in the day, Danny saw Delmar at a distance and rode to meet him. "Hello, Dry Bottle."

Delmar reined in his horse. "You talkin' to me?"

"Yeah, I am. Who the hell else would I be talkin' to? There ain't nobody else around."

Delmar sat quietly for a moment. "Danny, I don't want trouble, but if you're lookin' for a reason to start something, just get on with it. You'll be dead the minute you reach for your gun. And one more thing; I'm Mr. Delmar to you. Is that clear?"

Danny could not believe this was the same man, the man who had wandered the streets of Crooked Fork, begging for a drink. His first thought was to start trouble, to whip hell out of Delmar, but his good judgment prevailed. Delmar had a temper—he could kill a man without thinking twice.

"I don't mean to start no trouble, Delmar...Mr. Delmar."

"Then get out of my way and get back to pushin' cows."

Danny turned and rode back the way he came. As Delmar watched him go, he wondered, *How many more?* Damn John Roper. If he had not given John his word he could ride the other way. A thin smile came to Delmar's face. It felt good to be a man again. No more whiskey-filled nights for him, not ever. And for damn sure, those cows would be delivered somewhere in Kansas.

After two days of whooping, hollering, cussing, and downright hard riding, the trail herd began to take shape. John Roper rode into the main camp and sat down to coffee with Delmar and Bill Downs.

"Everything going okay?" he asked Delmar.

"Yeah, up to a point."

"I know what you mean," Roper responded quickly. "I had a talk with Ned Thompson. He was mad as hell but he'll get over it. I told him to let you be boss and for once in his life to leave things alone."

A worried look on his face, Bill Downs said to Delmar, "You got one bad man mad at you. He'll kill you some day if I know Ned."

"No, Bill, he won't kill me," Delmar corrected him. "He'll try. Then let the best man win."

"I got you some more men," Roper said. "They'll be here as soon as they can. Anything I can help you fellas with?"

"Not that I know of," Delmar said.

Bill shook his head.

"Well, I won't stay. I'd best be getting back."

"You can sleep in the supply wagon. I'll move out," Delmar suggested.

Roper started to protest, but Delmar left him stammering. He had already taken his gear out of the wagon.

"I'll flop down here by the fire. See you come daylight."

Bill and John talked by the fire more than a half hour before they, too, went to their bedrolls.

Delmar was up, saddled, and gone by first light. The cook watched him ride out, then banged his frying pan for breakfast. Bill Downs pulled on his boots, brushing the sleep from his eyes. He stood and stretched, cussed the night for being so short, and went to eat.

Expecting to find Roper and Delmar when he reached the chow line, he questioned the cook.

"Delmar rode out an hour ago. Roper ain't showed up yet," the cook informed him.

Bill went to the supply wagon. "You goin' to sleep all day, John?" he asked. There was no response. Bill pulled back the canvas cover. "Get up you lazy son of a bitch!" Roper did not move. Bill climbed into the wagon. The light was bad, but somehow he knew John Roper was dead.

"God Almighty," he whispered. Roper had been stabbed in the back in his sleep. *This'll cause one hell of a stink*, Bill thought.

"What do we do now?" he spoke aloud, half to himself and half to the cook.

"We got to take him back to town," the cook replied.

Bill nodded. "I'll get the wrangler to haul him back. Who would be so damn low as to stab John Roper in the back?" *Delmar had better know about this.* Bill's mind was working hard.

"Leave John's body in the wagon," he told the cook and the wrangler. Mounting the wrangler's horse, he hurried off in search of Delmar.

The ranchers had broken into three groups and Bill made for the first one he saw. Delmar had been there and gone. Bill found the second group a mile and a half down the trail. Delmar was just fixing to ride out when Bill caught up with him.

The trail boss sat his horse as Bill told him what had happened.

Delmar's muscular shoulders sagged, his rugged face white with shock.

"What do you make of it?" Bill asked.

Delmar swallowed hard, "God, I don't know. I didn't think they hated me enough to kill John. I'll go back to camp with you. I want to see that knife and look around."

"Sure, Del, let's ride."

There was nothing much to see. The knife was common enough. Delmar had seen a dozen or more like it. He combed through the wagon. Nothing. But somewhere, somehow, he had to find out who killed John Roper.

"Take him back to town," Delmar told the wrangler. "Make sure they bury him on his ranch."

Bill looked at Del questioningly.

"We got a herd to deliver," Delmar barked. "Today we lose all our extra help. That means we work twice as hard 'til we get more help. A rider could take a good three hours to circle the herd if he took his time and done it right. That includes keeping his eyes peeled for strays. It'll be hard to handle this size herd with twenty cowboys. But twenty'll just have to work more like forty, I guess."

▲▲▲

seven

Delmar could not get the murder off his mind. If there was any way on God's green earth to find out who killed John Roper, he would know before long.

The herd was starting to take shape. Delmar told the riders, "Keep 'em movin', don't push too hard. Just keep 'em walkin' north."

Danny Reed and six men were assigned from the Thompson brothers. Del approached them one at a time. Riding up alongside Danny, he commented, "Keep pushin', Danny. You're a little behind. I want one big herd by tonight, understand?" Danny nodded, and Del rode on.

Del watched for words or actions that might give him a clue, but there was nothing. The men worked hard that day, herding all the different brands together by nightfall. It was some herd, the biggest Del had ever seen. Bill Downs was everywhere, changing horses every four hours. He had just turned his fourth horse loose when Delmar rode into camp.

"I got the nighthawks lined up," Bill said as they both grabbed a plate and some hot coffee.

"Good," Del replied. "You see or hear anything?"

"No. Have you?"

"Not a damn word." Del sat cross-legged on the ground. Neither man spoke until they had finished eating. Del wiped his mouth with his hand. "I'll take the south side, and meet you on the west. I'd like to stay on the Colorado River for another ten days. It'll take us a little west, but the grass is good and by then we can handle 'em better."

Bill agreed, and Del mounted up and was gone.

It was late evening when Del and Bill met. Bone tired, they slid to the ground and each rolled a smoke.

"What do you know about Danny Reed?" Del asked.

"Been with the Thompsons a long time," Bill said. "You have a run-in with him?" He put his cigarette out with his boot toe.

"Yeah, you might say so," Del replied. "But I think he understands I'm boss now."

"See you in camp," Bill said over his shoulder as he swung into the saddle. He rode back the way he came.

Del cut through the herd. The cattle were not disturbed by the horse and rider. Del felt good about that. Nothing could spook them now except lightning, gunfire, or other loud noises.

The night passed too quickly for both men. It seemed they had just curled up in their bedrolls when the cook yelled, "Come and git it!"

"Today will make four days," Bill said. "We should be at least thirty-five to forty miles from Crooked Fork by nightfall."

"No more bright lights," Del replied.

"For many a day," Bill said. "I wasn't thinkin' about the bright lights; I was thinkin' about the distance. If we can average about ten miles a day..."

"That'd be too much to ask for," Del replied. "Better figure on six to eight. A herd this size can't move too fast. I'm goin' back to our last camp and have one more look around."

Del mounted up and headed south, back the way they had come. The sun was just peeping over the eastern horizon when he arrived. He dismounted and rolled a smoke, his eyes combing every inch of ground. As he reached the far side of the campground, Del turned, a move which saved his life. A rifle bullet tore through his shirtsleeve, just missing his arm. He dropped to the ground, pulling out his six-gun on the way down. It was no match for a rifle, but he was a long way from being dead. He waited for the next shot. A half hour went by. Nothing moved but his horse, quietly grazing some twenty yards away. Del scanned the trail behind him. There were plenty of places for a bushwacker to hide, even ride away without being seen. He decided that this one had done just that.

Del noticed a glint in the grass where the supply wagon had been. It was a stickpin with a small pearl on one end. He had never seen John Roper wear a stickpin. Then a thought came to him. The delicate pearl made him think it might belong to a woman. *A woman out here? Not likely.*

Del could not for the life of him think who would wear such a pin. He stared at it for a moment before fastening it to the front of his hat where everyone could see it. Maybe it would raise some questions.

Del rode slowly back to the herd. He decided not to mention the incident. He doubted that anyone would believe him anyway. But for damn sure, someone wanted him dead.

▲▲▲

eight

A wrangler who had hired on with John Roper only a few months before, Bobby Lee Norris arrived in Crooked Fork before sundown. He went to the sheriff's office and reported John Roper's murder. The news spread quickly and within half an hour a crowd of thirty people had gathered. Sheriff Will Bowman and Charlie, his deputy, were in their element, parading up and down the boardwalk answering questions.

Ned Thompson rode up. "Who done this?"

Sheriff Bowman said, "We don't know yet. This fella just brought him in."

Ned Thompson glanced toward Bobby Lee. "Did that old drunk pick a fight with Roper?"

"Not that I know of," Bobby Lee answered.

"Was Delmar around when this happened?" Ned demanded.

"Yes, he was there."

"Was he drunk?"

"No, he wasn't," Bobby Lee said.

"Who found him, then?"

"Bill Downs. He went to call Mr. Roper for breakfast and found him dead in his bedroll. Delmar rode out earlier."

"I bet a thousand he was the man who done it! It'd be just like 'im."

Sheriff Bowman nodded in agreement. "I'll get a few men together and ride out there in the mornin' and question the drunk—I mean—Mr. Delmar." He smiled slyly and everyone who heard him did likewise.

No one had forgotten who the drunk was and how he had gotten the biggest job in the county. To most, it was funny, but to some it was far from it. Anyone who would turn over a herd of seven thousand, six hundred cattle to a drunk and expect to get to Kansas must have taken leave of his senses. The man responsible was none other than John Roper, who now lay dead in the wagon on Main Street.

The local banker was almost in tears when he heard the news. "Oh, my God, this will ruin us all. So many people put cattle in this drive just because of John Roper. That miserable drunk can only fail."

Clem Paterson had been a banker some twenty years, and now his fortune depended on a drunk. Pacing the floor, he thought to himself, *Maybe I can get the ranchers to call a meeting and bring their cattle back.* Their ranches alone would not cover even a third of the notes outstanding without cattle. Loss of the cattle would break not only the ranchers, but the bank as well. He would rather die than face that possibility.

He left his office and walked toward the hotel. He spotted Sheriff Bowman talking to a crowd in front of the jail. There was no doubt about it. Will Bowman could talk the bark off a green tree. Now that he thought of it, Clem Paterson had never seen him do anything but talk. Well, he would have to do more than talk now.

Bowman, too, owed the bank: a thousand dollars. The note had been extended twice already, and his payments barely covered the interest. Paterson caught the sheriff's eye and they walked into his office.

Paterson explained his situation. "Sheriff, I want a meeting called tonight. I don't care if you and your deputy have to ride a horse to death getting the word around. I suggest you start within the next five minutes, or else this town will know just what shape your bank account is in. I can call in your note to boot. You won't even own the clothes you're wearing."

"I'll do it right now, Clem," Sheriff Bowman stammered. "God, don't call my note due. I'll do anything you say."

"Well, get movin'. As you go by, tell that man out there to go by the undertaker and bury John Roper. I'm sick of your politickin' ways. Now move." Sweat ran down Clem's face. He tried in vain to wipe it away with a handkerchief which was already soaking wet from previous use.

Sheriff Bowman came to a quick conclusion: if he wanted to keep on being sheriff of Clark County, he had best move promptly. Within half an hour Sheriff Bowman had men riding hellbent for leather in every direction.

It was a foolish move. The Merchants' Hardware clerk called it the last Paul Revere ride of the century. The ranchers could only gape in surprise as the riders galloped across their property shouting something about an emergency meeting at seven o'clock. Some commented that the damn war must have started all over again. Others thought the cattle drive had failed, or their cattle had died. Some even thought the town had burned down. By six o'clock the town was in complete turmoil. Who, what, where, and why had been asked a thousand times by six-thirty. By seven o'clock there was standing room only at the courthouse.

Clem Paterson sat on the judge's bench trying to quiet the crowd. Finally, Ned Thompson pulled out his gun and fired a hole in the ceiling. In the shocked silence which followed he snarled, "Now, damn it, listen to what Clem here has to say!"

Clem cleared his throat. "The reason I called this meeting is to explain the situation, the position of First National Bank, and the position of you folks as ranchers. To those of you who don't know, John Roper is dead. He was murdered in his sleep out on the trail. John put his word, his ranch, and his cattle on the line. He backed this cattle drive. Well, who's backing it now? It's bein' run by the town drunk who's not used to bein' responsible for anything except another drink. If he fails to deliver the herd, you'll all go broke and I'll be forced to call in your notes. Where does that leave you ranchers?" Clem sat down. He must have found a dry handkerchief somewhere because he was wiping the sweat from his face and brow.

The crowd murmured, and from the back of the room a rancher yelled, "What can we do about it?"

"That's up to you," Clem replied evenly. "I strongly suggest you put someone responsible in charge, or bring the cattle back, and sell them a few at a time like we've done in the past."

Ned Thompson took charge of the meeting. "I think we better git our cows back, then if we decide to continue the drive we can put someone else in charge." Ned waited a few minutes. "Well, all in favor say *Aye*." The vote was unanimous.

Ned said, "We'll leave in the mornin'. Send a couple of men from each ranch. We'll rendezvous where we met for the drive."

The meeting broke up without Sheriff Bowman saying a word. Clem Paterson passed the sheriff on his way out the door. "Sheriff, I want you to to go along, and don't send anybody else, just in case there might be trouble."

"If that drunk gives us any trouble," Bowman said, "I'll arrest him on suspicion of murder. That'll cool him off."

Clem Paterson nodded. "Now you're thinkin' straight."

Sheriff Bowman was proud of himself. He was back in the good graces of the banker. Just then, Nellie Howard burst through the door. Nellie had been widowed for nearly three years. Her husband was killed breaking horses for John Roper. "What's goin' on?" she demanded, looking Will Bowman straight in the eye. She was every cowboy's dream: five-foot-four, 130 pounds, topped with shoulder-length brown hair and snapping dark eyes.

Bowman began to explain. "There's nothin' to get excited

about. Everything's under control."

"I didn't ride all the way in here to listen to a bull-roarin', fat hog. I want some answers." She pushed past Bowman and caught Paterson's arm as he was leaving.

Still mopping his brow, Clem Paterson repeated his concerns about Delmar and the herd. "There ain't no use gettin' into this thing, Mrs. Howard. You're not in debt to the bank."

Nellie took a step back. "You're worse than that fat-bellied sheriff. I got cattle on that drive like everybody else, but you're only concerned about your money. You ain't worried about nobody but your bank. I ain't forgotten, Clem Paterson; you turned me down for a loan. Well, I got the money. So you and your precious money can go to hell!" She turned on her heel and left Clem Paterson staring after her. He wondered where she got the loan. She had promised never to tell anyone and, so far, Nellie had kept her promise.

▲▲▲

nine

Nellie's sister, Teresa Stoneman, was also widowed, at the early age of twenty-six. Teresa's husband had been killed in the war and she had never remarried. Together they managed the ranch, surviving high taxes and the ravages of nature. Fortunately, they had no mortgage since Bill Howard had paid cash for the ranch before he was killed.

Nellie and Teresa had put a thousand head in the herd, all the cattle they could round up with the aid of old Uncle Ted. Ted was well up in years when he went to work for Bill Howard. By the time Bill was killed, he was considered a member of the family. He figured it was his job to look after Nellie and Teresa. As foreman, he was responsible for the hiring and firing.

Uncle Ted was proud of his job. Only the Howards knew his real name. He was born in Beaumont, Texas, the son of the proud and God-fearing Judge Clayton Jennings. Ted ran away from home at the age of seventeen after a bitter quarrel with his father. He had never returned. After a time, he was too ashamed to return, particularly after learning of his parents' deaths. He lived with his guilt. He had told no one except Bill Howard who kept his secret in life as well as death.

The years had slipped by. The Howard spread had become his home and would be until he died.

People on the Howard spread kept to themselves and did not bother anyone. Nor did they want to be bothered. But under the circumstances, Nellie figured she had a perfect right to know what was taking place on the drive to Kansas.

The ranchers' rendezvous looked more like the annual governor's picnic or a Fourth of July celebration with Quantrell as the guest of honor. No one had seen so many guns since the battle of Bull Run and there was enough yelling and cussing and he-man threats made to elect a congressman. Finally, declaring that everyone had gone crazy, Ned Thompson asserted that only a few men were needed.

Nellie Howard piped up. "You might be the big bull o' the woods at your ranch, but me and Uncle Ted are goin' to check on the herd. It's a free country and we're not waitin' around to be picked by some big mouth."

She cast a fierce look at Sheriff Bowman. "We're leaving right now." And she and Uncle Ted left the crowd staring at their backsides as they rode away.

"I'll be damned," Clem Peterson said. "I would've never believed it."

Ben Thompson spit a stream of tobacco juice between his horse's ears. "I tell you one thing, I wouldn't want to tangle with them. They're true Texans, by God."

Sheriff Bowman did not like the idea of womenfolk getting involved. He meant to bring Dry Bottle Delmar in for trial. That would stop all the hell-raising around Crooked Fork and Clark County. But somehow he got the feeling that Nellie Howard would get in his way.

As they rode away, Uncle Ted worked his horse closer to Nellie and said, "You expecting trouble?"

Nellie smiled. "No, Ted, I don't think there'll be any trouble, but just in case, we'll be on the right side."

Ted did not know what she meant, but he trusted Nellie to do the right thing. However, he did worry about what might happen if Dry Bottle did not keep his promise to John Roper. In the past, John Roper had always been right, even, so far, about the trail drive.

Ted wiped his face with his bandana. He had come to the conclusion that Nellie was not interested in the trail drive. She was confident that it was going well. But she was interested in John Roper's death. That was her reason for making the trip. Ted eased himself in his saddle, took a drink from his canteen, then hung it back on his saddle. If he was any judge of character, Nellie Howard would find the answer, and then all hell would break loose, no matter where she found it. Whether it was on the trail, up town, or back at the spread, Nellie would see that justice was done.

Ted's mind drifted to the Thompson brothers. The talk on the range was not good. They had tried to put a cattle drive together themselves. Their stated reason was to get money for everyone, but the real reason was their large note at the bank. And it was Clem Paterson who had put the pressure on the brothers to make a drive. But without John Roper's authority and know-how, it would still be just talk. The whole thing was John Roper's doing.

Ted reined his horse in. Nellie had stopped.

"Shall we eat a bite?" she asked.

"Yeah, I could stand a bite. I was plumb daydreamin'."

"I doubt that. I never seen you daydreamin', but I would say you got everything figured out by now." Nellie took their lunch out of the saddlebag.

Ted dismounted. "No, not yet, but I'm workin' on it," he admitted. "I somehow got the idea you're the one with all the answers in this-here puzzle."

Serious, Nellie looked up with a slight frown. "I wish I did, Ted. I wish I did."

They ate in silence, lost in their own thoughts.

"We best ride if we want to stay ahead of that bunch from town. I never seen so much nonsense in one place in my life. They had enough guns to start a war. I really can't see the reason for all the concern. Bill Downs is with the drive, and there ain't a better cowman alive."

"That's my way of lookin' at it." Nellie nodded her agreement. Then she mounted up. "Come on, slow poke. We best get some miles on us or that herd will be in Kansas before we catch 'em."

Ted slowly climbed into the saddle. "I wish they were. It would sure stop a lot of ridin'. "

In three days on the trail they had seen no one. Finally, on the fourth day, at noon, they saw the dust of the herd. Although they were covered with dust, at Nellie's insistence they rode with the drag riders until the herd was circled for the night.

They found Delmar and Bill Downs at the chuck wagon just before dark.

"Well, hello." Delmar quickly stood and removed his hat. "This is an unexpected visit."

Bill Downs did likewise and they both shook hands with Uncle Ted.

"You're makin' good time," Nellie commented. "The cattle look good. And Delmar, I believe you're getting fat." She winked at Bill Downs.

"What brings you way out here?" Delmar asked.

"Well, to start with, we're really sorry about John," Nellie said. "Another thing, there's a whole passel of men behind us. They'll probably be here in the mornin'. Ned Thompson, Sheriff Bowman, and Clem Paterson will be with them."

Delmar was silent, and Bill Downs looked up with a frown.

"They're comin' to take the herd back to town."

Neither man spoke and Nellie continued. "They don't think Delmar here is capable of bossing this drive. They're afraid he'll start drinking again. At least that's their excuse. Clem Paterson has them convinced they'll lose their ranches and the bank will go broke. So it comes down to this: they don't trust Delmar or you." Nellie nodded at Bill.

After a moment of silence, Delmar asked, "What do you think, Nellie?"

"I don't think, I know. If there's a way, this side of the hot place, you and Bill will do it. However, there is something you should know. Tell 'em Ted."

Ted pushed the hat back on his graying head. "Well, it's like this. Once a ship gets so far out to sea, the captain becomes judge and jury. He is the law. It's the same with a cattle drive. You, Delmar, are the law. You say whether these cattle go back or not. If you say they go to the railhead, that's the law. But if your crew quits, there's nothing you can do. Every man has a free choice. You're on federal land now, have been since yesterday, guessin' at the miles. So the choice is up to you."

Delmar stood up and threw the cold coffee out of his cup. He and Bill Downs went to their horses.

"I'll find out about the small ranchers. No sense askin' the Thompson crew," Bill said as he mounted up.

Delmar nodded. "I'll see you later." And they rode off into the night.

Ted and Nellie watched them go. "What do you think his decision will be?" Ted asked.

Nellie answered over her shoulder, "I don't know, but whatever it is, we're with him all the way."

"I figured that much," Ted said. "I know one thing. I sure don't want him agin me. Did you see the look in Delmar's eyes as we were talkin'? Damned if that look wouldn't scare the horns off a range bull!"

"Come on, Ted, let's get some sleep."

Ted stood and stretched. "Sure, Nellie." Somehow he could not get the look in Delmar's eyes out of his mind.

Ted jumped to a sitting position as the cook banged on the frying pan. Whatever he had been dreaming was instantly forgotten. *Who the hell heard of bangin' a pan in a man's ear to wake him up?* As Ted pulled on his boots, Nellie was already up and about.

There was no sign of Bill Downs or Delmar. Ted got some coffee, bacon, and a biscuit.

Nellie approached him and said, "Let's saddle up and have a look around."

As they rode the herd's east flank, they saw the town crowd coming. They turned their horses in that direction and a quarter mile west of them, a half-dozen other riders did the same. Ted counted twenty men with the sheriff, a good quarter mile behind the herd. Delmar's crew numbered eleven.

▲▲▲

ten

Ned Thompson greeted the rider. "Well, I guess you know why we're here. I see the Howards' pup has already told you."

Ted stiffened in his saddle. He was fighting mad. No son of a bitch had the right to call him a dog.

"Easy, Ted," Nellie whispered. "A fight is what they want. Let Delmar speak."

"You, Mr. Delmar, are under arrest for suspicion of murder in the death of John Roper." Sheriff Bowman continued. "And I expect you to come along peaceful."

Delmar remained silent.

Nellie looked around. Bill Downs was nowhere to be seen.

"Well, to start off with, Sheriff," Delmar said, loud enough for all to hear, "you can go to hell. And Ned, there are only three other ranchers who agree with you. Hear me, and hear me good. I am the law here. I could shoot you down, every one of you, for trying to take my herd. Considering the circumstances, I won't. But I won't stop this herd, not one day. I am willing to cut your cattle out as we go. It might take ten days, so Ned, be prepared to start gatherin' your cows."

Whiskey, Guns & Cows

Delmar turned his horse and went back the way he had come.

"You dirty lowlife drunk!" Ned Thompson exploded. "I swore I'd kill you if you ever spoke to me again." He raised a rifle to his shoulder and took aim at Delmar's back. A rifle shot echoed across the river. Ned Thompson crumpled, pain and shock contorting his face. He fell from the saddle, face down in the dust.

Clem Paterson was the first to reach him. He was still alive, unconscious, and rapidly losing blood. As it rammed through his shoulder, the bullet had broken his collarbone, leaving a mean-looking hole where it came out.

"Best we get him bandaged up and to a doctor," Clem said.

Glaring at Delmar's distant, retreating form, the sheriff swore, "Damn him to hell, anyway. He had us all set up."

"What did you expect?" Phil Lacross, a rancher from the south side of town said. "You don't think he rode out here bold as Caesar to say, 'Here I am, shoot me,' do you? He might be a drunk, but he ain't stupid."

"He'll pay the price, damn him. I swear it!"

Angry, Phil Lacross shot back, "Frankly, I think it was a damn stupid move on Ned's part. Don't you realize that Ned was goin' to shoot Delmar in the back? What the hell do you call that, Sheriff? I call it cold-blooded murder. Damned if I'll be part of any such thing. If you was worth a shit, you'd arrest Ned Thompson."

Some of the other ranchers agreed with Phil.

"I've never seen the like in all my fifty years. There ain't a damn thing stoppin' you from joinin' Delmar," Clem Paterson said with disgust. "Only remember, if you do, I'll call in every last one of your notes."

"You, Mr. Banker, can go to hell! Delmar never done me and mine no wrong. I'm joinin' up with him right now if he'll let me." Phil pulled his horse around. "And one more thing. If one of you brave yellow bellies shoots me in the back, my kinfolk will ride you down and kill every last one of you."

Three other ranchers followed Phil Lacross as he made his way toward the herd.

They were met a hundred yards from the drags by Delmar and Bill Downs.

"We come to join up, if you'll have us," Lacross said. "We don't cotton to cold-blooded murder, and that was what Ned Thompson was fixin' to do. He had a bead on you, Delmar."

Bill scowled. "How do we know they didn't send you over here?"

"You don't," Lacross admitted. "But I tell you this, if we don't ride with you, we're done anyway. Clem Paterson promised to call our notes due and payable. If you don't make it, we're all done."

Delmar nodded. "Okay, Phil. Bill here is the ramrod. You'll answer to him. But remember, I want the Thompson brothers' cattle cut out of this herd. Leave them where the hell ever. We can use the extra help."

"Do you really want to do this, Delmar? You know it'll force the Thompsons to make their own drive."

"That's right," Delmar said. "The feed will be short and I hope they have to hire fifty men just to keep up. Any objections?"

Phil Lacross smiled. "Not a damn one. If a man tried to kill me, I guess I'd be mad as hell, too."

Bill Downs nodded. "Let's head north. We got a long way to go."

▲▲▲

eleven

Danny Reed could not believe his ears. "I'll be damned! You mean I'm to come along behind you and pick up the Thompsons' cows?"

"We don't give a damn one way or the other. I imagine you'll hear from Ben Thompson shortly," Delmar replied.

"Ned was hurt pretty bad," Bill Downs said.

Fire in his eyes, Danny demanded, "Who shot Ned?"

"Well, let's just say somebody stopped a murder."

"I see," Danny said. "I'll pass the word to my crew. We'll drop back and wait for orders."

Bill and Delmar rode on. "Do you think he'll give us any trouble?" Bill asked.

"I really don't think so," Delmar said. "He'll be too busy trying to gather up a scattered-out herd."

The word was out: to cut out all Thompson cattle, if and when it was convenient, and leave them behind. The men smiled as they were told. By nightfall everyone knew of the *big split*, as they called it. Tommy Cline, a B-Bar drover commented, "You can bet the button on your underwear flap that this shindig is far from over."

Whiskey, Guns & Cows

As Delmar and Bill rode on, Bill said, "Gee Klist, boss, he might be right!"

Delmar turned in his saddle and looked at Bill. "Have you lost your mind or are you speakin' Chinese now?"

"Someday I'll tell you what I'm talkin' about. You was still drunk when it happened."

"What happened?" Delmar asked.

"You don't know it, my good man, but you damn near turned out to be a Chinaman." Bill Downs rode off, leaving Delmar with a puzzled look on his face.

Nellie and Uncle Ted were eating when Bill and Delmar rode into camp. "We dropped about four hundred head of Thompson cows. We've been workin' the drags makin' sure they're dropped first." There was a twinkle in Nellie's eyes. "You're one smart man, Delmar. I would've bet my hat pin you'd put up a fight!"

Stunned, Delmar abruptly turned away. "I didn't know you owned one," he replied over his shoulder.

"You'd be surprised at what I own," Nellie replied.

"Yes, I suppose I would," he said, sitting down with his plate.

Nellie pointed at his hat. "See, you own one."

"One what?" Delmar asked.

"A hat pin."

"Uh, yeah. I found this one just a few days ago."

Nellie continued. "There ain't too many people wear them nowadays. I was just tryin' to remember who I seen wear one not too long ago. It looked like the one you're wearin'."

Delmar kept his attention on his food. "If you happen to think of it, I'd sure like to know."

Nellie looked at him. "You mean that, don't you?"

Delmar sipped his coffee. "Yeah, just curious, I guess." Delmar did not want to push the issue any further.

But Nellie was persistent. "That pin means quite a bit to you, don't it?"

"You might say that," Delmar replied.

"Does it belong to a girl somewhere?"

Delmar shook his head.

"Was you ever married?"

"Yes, I lost my family up on the Missouri-Kansas line. Some damn general gave the order: move or else."

"I heard about that order, number eleven, I believe they called it."

"That's the one," Delmar agreed. "I never got around to doin' no courtin' since then. I been too busy tryin' to drink myself to death."

Nellie turned toward him. "At least you're honest. I had quite a time after my husband was killed. My whole world fell in. I even thought of commitin' suicide but I didn't have the courage. But as somebody once said, time heals all wounds. Guess mine is pretty well healed. I seldom think about him anymore."

"It's surprisin'," Delmar admitted. "I seldom think of my family either. I guess I'm too busy."

Nellie reached out and touched his cheek. "Good night, Delmar. I want you to know I believe in you." She rose to her feet and left him gazing after her.

A strange feeling came over him. He had not said that many words to a woman in a long time.

The morning brought a bright new day. Delmar found himself worrying about the Thompson cattle. *What if...*, he thought. *Oh, to hell with what if. If Bill Downs had missed Ned Thompson, I'd be buried and forgotten by now.* Swinging his horse around, he went to the rear of the herd where Nellie, Uncle Ted, and two other cowboys were cutting out Thompson cattle. Delmar helped for a while, then took a ride down the back trail where Danny Reed, the Thompsons' cow boss, and his crew were rounding up the cattle. Their herd was already beginning to take shape.

The cutting of the Thompson cattle was going much smoother than he had expected. At this rate, the Thompsons would have all of their cattle within a week. Delmar watched them work for half an hour. Danny Reed was doing exactly what he would do under the circumstances.

Delmar was about to leave when three riders came into view. They were coming from the wrong direction to be part of the Thompson crew. Approaching the small herd, they stopped to talk to some of the crew. After a short time, they rode away down the back trail toward the river. A wild thought occurred to Delmar: *Could these be some of the men John Roper had promised? Or did John get himself murdered before he had a chance to hire anyone?*

Curiosity brought Delmar to a crazy decision. There was only one way to know. Knowing John Roper, he had the men hired before he left town. And according to John Roper, extra help should have arrived by then. Putting spurs to his horse, Delmar rode wide of the river, picking out a place where he could intercept the three men, about a mile and a half from the Thompson herd.

Delmar pushed his horse hard and some two hours later found himself ahead of the three men. He stopped and waited. He began to wish he had not run his horse so hard. But he needed to get ahead of the three men if he was to have the advantage, just in case he was wrong. After waiting for some time, he was about to give up, when his thoughts were rudely interrupted.

"Señor, if you will just get down from that horse, I won't kill you."

Delmar could not believe he was at their mercy. Slowly he dismounted.

"Please, Mr. Mans, step away from you horse. He is a good one."

"Damn," Delmar swore under his breath. Whoever these people were, they were not ordinary cowhands. The one doing the talking was Mexican, as sure as hell. Now he would be stripped of his guns, horse, saddle, and all. He would be lucky if they left him his boots.

"Please, señor, turn around so we can see what kind of gringo you are."

Delmar turned around. He still could not see his captor, who was partially hidden behind some tall brush.

"Tell me, señor, what is it they call you?"

"Delmar's the name. I'm the boss of the Roper herd, on ahead some six or eight miles."

"Tell me, señor, what was you planning to do?"

"I was plannin' on askin' you some questions."

"What questions, señor?"

"Was you hired by John Roper about a week or ten days ago?"

"Señor, please drop your gun belt."

Delmar unbuckled his belt and let it drop. He was sure he would either be dead or the laughingstock of the whole country.

"Step back, señor."

As Delmar stepped back, a tall Mexican showed himself smiling. He came forward with an outstretched hand."

Delmar stared in disbelief. "By God, Jingo? I can't believe it's really you!"

"Oh, yes, Mr. Delmar. You were my major too long to forget." The two men embraced.

"Come my friends, come," Jingo called to his men.

They were all Mexicans or mixed blood, and they were armed to the teeth."

"They told us there was no Roper herd. They said it was the..." Jingo hesitated.

"Thompson," Delmar said.

"Right, right. Where is Captain John?"

"Dead," Delmar answered. Then he went on to tell his good friend what happened.

Jingo pointed to Delmar's hat. "Tell me, why do you wear the sign of one of us?"

Delmar looked up quickly. "I don't understand."

"Major, the pin."

Then Delmar realized that Jingo's friends each wore a stickpin just like the one he had found. *What does it stand for?* he wondered. *Did John Roper belong to some secret organization?*

"Señor, you can speak up. These are my *amigos*. We have been together ever since we crossed the border into Mexico."

Delmar grinned. "I see. But did you know John Roper was killed with a knife in the back while he slept?"

Jingo rolled himself a corn husk cigarette before he replied. "That makes you very, how you say it?"

"Cautious," Delmar replied.

Jingo nodded. "Señor, me and my men would never kill Señor Roper. He give us money and shelter even after they run us out of Mexico."

Delmar picked up his gun and strapped it on.

"Hey, *amigos*," Jingo shouted to his friends. "Thees one, he shoot Crazy Bill Anderson. Don't try shooting him, my friends. He will kill you quick. Are you still quick?" Jingo asked.

Delmar nodded.

"I not forget, *amigo,* when you shoot that army major. He die pretty quick."

Delmar knew if he let Jingo talk, his secret would be out. That alone could get him killed. He was wanted by the Union Army. That damn major had raped his wife and was responsible for the death of his whole family. Some called it war; Delmar called it getting even. Maybe two wrongs did not make a right, but it sure made him feel like a man again.

"Jingo, I'd like your help. But if you say one more word about me and that major, you'll kiss the devil with your second breath. Do you understand?"

"*Si*, señor, I understand. In Mexico we talk, but not here."

"And one more thing, if you cause me any trouble, you're one dead Mexican. I want this herd delivered and they're goin' to be, as long as there's breath in my body. If you know anything about John Roper's death, I want to know about it now."

Jingo threw up his hands. "I know nothing, señor. John Roper, he was my captain, my friend. If I know who kill him, I will kill him myself. Señor, if you have cows to drive, we will help you. These friends of mine are just a little lazy, but I think they work for you okay."

Delmar looked Jingo straight in the eye. "Okay, Jingo, let's go drive cows."

Jingo smiled. "Señor Delmar, you are one good man. Nothing will happen to you, my men will see to that. This one, he can't talk, but he can hear real good."

Delmar looked the man over. His black eyes were clear and quick. He was about thirty-five and a good six feet tall. Delmar noticed the way he wore his gun, pushed back further than most. In front of his gun, he wore a knife, smaller than a Bowie, but larger than most.

"Can he throw that?" Delmar asked, pointing to the knife.

Jingo chuckled. "Like you with your gun, señor."

Bill Downs was surprised when Delmar showed up with three Mexicans. "Where the hell have you been, boss? Have you been to Mexico and back since mornin'?"

Delmar introduced Jingo and his friends. "This is your boss," Delmar told them. "This one can't talk, Bill. Jingo will do the talkin' for him, but he can hear damn good."

Bill always spoke his mind. This time was no exception. "I somehow never trusted a knife-throwin' Mexican," he said.

"What side of the fence did you fight on, Bill?" Delmar asked.

"I was a Johnny Reb, by God." Bill dug his heels in, just in case anyone dared question him.

"So was he," Delmar asserted. "So don't make snap judgments 'til you know all the facts. I was Jingo's major."

"*Si,* señor, he was that and quick he shoot, too." Jingo realized he had said enough, and stood waiting for a reply.

Bill's shoulders relaxed. "Damn you, Delmar. Why don't you tell me what's goin' on? Then I won't have to show my fightin' feathers."

Jingo grinned. "Señor Bill, we will get along. I think you are one damn good John Reb!"

The cook ladled stew into Jingo's plate. "This ain't *frijoles,* but it'll fill you up."

"Señor Cook, I don't miss the beans, as you call them, only the peppers. I have some in my saddlebags I will share with you."

"No, thanks. I remember one time we didn't have no brandin' irons when we was workin' in the panhandle. Well, sir, them Mexicans had some hot peppers. They boiled them up, put the juice on them cows, and them brands showed up like none you ever seen. The hair never did grow back on them cows."

Jingo laughed. "Señor, I think you bullshit a little. But if you want to see trouble, put my peppers in the horses' grain. Señor, no one wants to ride 'em."

"Damned if the first liar ain't got a chance!" Bill Downs exclaimed.

Nellie and Uncle Ted accepted the Mexicans, and the rest of the crew soon learned they were superb ropers. They used the long, braided rawhide riatas. Bill Downs decided to take a few lessons from the mute.

"How come you picked the mute for a teacher, Bill?" Shorty Driedon asked.

"Cause he can't say a damn word if I make a mistake."

▲▲▲

twelve

The drive was already twenty days out and Danny Reed could no longer see the dust of the Roper herd. Danny was not happy with his orders from Ben Thompson. He had been told in no uncertain terms to leave the Roper herd alone.

"There's no damn sense in fightin' that drunk," Ben had said. "After we get these cattle to market, then we'll settle with him. For now, you follow his example and get these cows to market.

"We can't help what happened to Ned. Besides, he went out here half-crazy with the banker, thinkin' they could scare that drunk into just rollin' over and playin' dead. John Roper knew his men, 'cause from what I see, he's doin' a hell of a job. You'll do well to watch and learn from him.

"You're in charge of the Thompson herd. That gives you the same power he has over his herd. Now I want cows to market, not a bunch of shootin' and horse play. If I hear you startin' a shootin' war, I'll kill you myself, you understand? If you want this job, do as I say."

Danny had made up his mind. He would not start anything, but no law said he had to help anyone either. His supplies were slow in coming. The wait for supplies slowed them down two days. He had everything he could think of except salt. Why Delmar insisted on salt, he did not know. No one in his right mind freighted salt anywhere.

They were some five days behind the Roper herd. They had left the river and were trailing on dry feed. One pass over the dry grass and it was gone. Danny was forced to trail to one side of the Roper herd. Two herds that close together left a strip of bare ground a mile wide. If water was short, they would just have to make do. No way around it, the Thompson herd would be considerably lighter when they got to market.

The Thompson point rider reported unshod horse tracks. That meant only one thing: Indians. Danny wondered what they would do if they were attacked by a bunch of Indians. *Should we stop and fight, or keep up with the herd? What if the herd stampedes?* He had never seen a stampede in a herd that size. A hundred questions went through his mind daily. If only he knew what to expect.

Danny also noticed that his men were becoming more and more irritable. Twice he had to break up a fight. He even found himself getting short-tempered. God only knew what it would be like in sixty days.

Danny's reverie was shattered as he looked up. The four left-flank riders came riding hellbent for leather toward him. Danny spurred his horse to meet them.

"What do you want us to do, boss?" Larry Coleman asked. "We got twenty painted hellions over there wantin' some of our herd."

"How many?" Danny asked.

"I told you, twenty of them. Are you hard of hearin'?"

"No, damn it! I mean how many cows do they want?"

"Hell, they made signs, like half of 'em."

Danny and the men rode toward the Indians. On his way, he picked up two more men. Maybe a show of force would change their minds. It was just as Larry Coleman had said. There were twenty of them. Danny did not recognize the tribe or understand the language, but when they made their sign, he shook his head *no*.

They were poorly armed. Danny was sure if shooting started, they would be short quite a few braves in just a few minutes. They made signs for half an hour, but Danny held his ground. Finally, Danny held up both hands, meaning ten and no more.

"See that one with all the black paint on his face? I think he's the big bull. If they start shootin', I'll get him first."

"Don't bet on it, Coleman. They ain't goin' to set there like ducks in a pond."

After a few minutes it was agreed: ten cows. Danny motioned toward the back of the herd. The riders cut out ten head of the drags, leaving them behind.

"How many times do we have to do this?" Danny asked Coleman.

"Damned if I know. If we do this every day, we won't have no cows to trail."

Somehow Danny knew he had done the right thing, but his instinct told him to put a double guard on their horses that night. A horse was an Indian's pride and joy, and he had heard many stories of thievery. The night passed uneventfully.

The next day promised to be just as hot as the day before. Danny cast his eyes to the horizon. No sign of clouds.

The cook complained, "I thought it was supposed to rain in the springtime? If we don't git some rain pretty soon, we're in big trouble."

"Speakin' of trouble, if any of those redskins come around today, no cows. We're not givin' cows away every day." As Danny saddled up a horse, in the back of his mind he knew where he was going. He had to talk to someone and Delmar was the man. He rode out, leaving the herd behind.

By eleven o'clock he was riding in the dust of the Roper herd. Suddenly, a riata whistled over his head, and before he had a chance to defend himself, he was jerked from his horse and dragged along the ground. Arms pinned tightly to his sides, he had no way to draw his gun. As he wriggled helplessly, someone grasped him by his shoulders, pulling him to his feet. Dazed, Danny did not realize his gun had been removed, but he felt the burn of the rope as his hands and legs were tied.

"What the hell are you doin'?" he asked. "I came to see Delmar."

As he lay hog-tied on the ground, Danny looked up to see his captor, a Mexican, smiling down at him. It was one of the same bunch he had told to get lost a few days back. The Mexican tied Danny across his horse. Danny's cussing and yelling did not change a thing. As he was led around the herd at a run, he found it hard to cuss and breathe at the same time. After a good hour, they stopped.

"What have we here?" Delmar asked.

Proud of himself, the Mexican just smiled.

"Well, I'll be damned. Come here, Bill."

"Damn it, Delmar, tell this fool Mexican who I am!" Danny demanded.

Bill Downs stepped forward. "Well Danny, haven't you learned to ride? First time I ever seen you tied to a horse. You look like a Chinaman I seen one time. Gee Klist, boss, let's cut him loose and see if he can walk."

"That dirty Mexican dog could get himself killed treating people like that!"

"You be careful what you call him," Bill said sharply. "It just so happens that he works for me."

Red-faced, Danny fought to control his temper. "Okay, but hell, all I wanted to do was talk."

Delmar looked at Bill. Bill shook his head. "Well you're here. I guess we should apologize for our man roughin' you up. What do you want to talk about?"

Bill took the gun from the Mexican mute and gave it back to Danny.

"Have you seen any Indians?"

"Sure we seen 'em."

"Did they want any cows?"

"Yes, they wanted a few. We give 'em a few. If you don't they'll steal 'em," Bill concluded.

"Will they jump your herd?" Danny asked.

"Sometimes they will. The Kiowa ain't bad, but Southern Cheyennes are hell for that."

"How do you tell one from another?"

Two or three of Delmar's men laughed.

"Well, what we seen so far is Kiowa."

"Did one of 'em have black paint on?" Danny asked.

Bill stepped forward. "Was he marked like this?" Bill drew a picture in the dirt.

"Yes."

"Well, you got off lucky. How many cows did you give him?"

"Ten," Danny said.

"Did he take 'em and leave?"

"Yes."

"He'll be back. That's old Walkin' Bird himself. He don't like whites. Worse yet, he don't like us crossin' his land. He's never been known to make exceptions."

Everyone nodded in agreement.

"And furthermore, he'll steal something before he's through."

"Why don't somebody kill him?" Danny asked.

"Can you whip two or three hundred mad Indians? This whole damn country would come down on you. Walkin' Bird is chief of all the Cheyenne down here. When he steals something from someone who crosses his land, he considers they paid the price, and he didn't lose any warriors. Kinda hard to understand, but that's the way it is."

The supply wagon drove up and Nellie jumped out. "Well, what is this, some kind of club meetin'?"

Danny removed his hat. "Howdy, ma'am. No, just askin' a few questions."

"He's got old Walkin' Bird breathin' down his neck," Delmar told her.

"Oh, did you lose any men?" she asked.

"Not yet, ma'am. But this is my first time with a trail drive and sometimes it pays to ask questions."

Nellie winked at Delmar, "Well, I'm sure Delmar and Bill can answer your questions." She went back to the wagon.

"Well, I best be gettin' back."

"Ride a ways with him," Bill told the mute, "so he won't be gettin' tied up again."

Danny mounted up. He did not like being escorted away from the Roper herd, but he did not want to be roughed up again. Somewhere in the dust of the drags, he looked around and found himself riding alone again. Somewhere the Mexican had left him, quiet as a panther cat.

That damn Delmar has all the answers, Danny thought. *Why in hell couldn't the Thompson brothers hire Delmar to make their drive? No, that damn banker had to ruin everything.* Danny would just as soon have been working the ranch herd with a bunkhouse bed every night, a drink or two on Saturday night, and a weekly trip to the local whorehouse to calm his nerves. *My God, how long will it be before I find a drink, let alone a woman?*

No more trail drives for him. It was just too much—being forced to go to his enemy for advice, no less.

▲▲▲

thirteen

Danny's horse pricked up its ears. Looking ahead, Danny saw a huge cloud of dust. "God Almighty, I'm in trouble again!" As he put spurs to his horse, he heard rifle shots. It was plain to see what was happening. Danny reached for his own rifle.

Walking Bird had attacked just as Delmar said. The Indians had cut a hundred head from the main herd and the drovers were putting up a good fight. Danny had no choice but to help his men. He raised his rifle, aimed, and a brave out in front of him fell dead. Another brave turned to ride back the way he had come. He never made it. As Danny fired, the Indian's horse went down and the Indian, bleeding from a head wound, fell in a heap.

The shooting had stopped. Danny continued toward the herd, looking for signs of his men. He found three hidden behind some rocks.

"They hit us from all sides," Coleman said. "Damn it, boss, we had to do something. We shot back and I got that black-faced son of a bitch just like I told you."

Danny suddenly felt sick.

"You don't look well," Coleman said.

Danny walked slowly to his horse. He stood for a full minute, his mind racing. *Delmar, you son of a bitch, you were right. Now I got no choice. I need your help again, not to save this damn herd, but to save me and my men from total destruction. Why didn't Chief Walkin' Bird raid Delmar's herd instead?"*

Danny had made up his mind. Even Ben Thompson had said it. There was nothing wrong with Delmar. He had brains, plenty of cow savvy, and he knew the country. And for damn sure he knew about Indians. Delmar, as far as Danny was concerned, was the salvation of both herds. If he could manage to persuade Delmar to combine the herds again and get them to Kansas, never again would he have a bad word to say against him. *God, I have said plenty,* Danny admitted to himself.

He mounted his horse and turned to his men. "I'm goin' back to camp, or what's left of it, and get a fresh horse. You get these cattle rounded up. I don't think Walkin' Bird's bunch will be back today. They went to get some help, and that's just what I'm goin' to do."

"You goin' to the Roper herd?" Coleman asked. "Hell, man, they'll throw you out on your ear!"

"Let me tell you something. I'm goin' to see Delmar, Bill Downs, and anyone else who will listen. You shot the chief of the Cheyennes, that one with the black on his face. He always steals a few cows but nobody gets hurt. He did it to save face with his people and you shot him dead. Now it'll be hell to pay. If I could just roll back the last few hours I'd shoot you, Coleman, so help me I would. You've upset the shit cart. We'll be lucky to get out of this alive. So don't tell me where to go. You'd better git these cattle rounded up and damn quick. I'll be back some time tonight. Now, damn it, move!"

He left the men gaping in amazement. It was the first time Danny had ever spoken his mind. Before he had always quietly straddled the fence, but now it was plain to see he was going to ask Delmar, the town drunk, for help.

Coleman said, "Thompson won't like this one bit."

Texas Bob, a one-eyed puncher, fixed the patch over his bad eye, squinted into the sun and replied, "You know something, right now Danny doesn't give a shit what anybody likes. He needs help and he's man enough to go get it. If Thompson don't like what he's doin', tell the dumb bastard to come ask me. I'll tell 'im where the bear shits in the woods." He strode off in search of his horse.

Danny knew better than to ride in quietly. As he sang some long-forgotten song, he was cut off on a sour note. Once again the smiling Mexican appeared from out of nowhere and blocked the trail in front of him. Danny threw up his hands and the Mexican escorted him into camp.

The evening shadows were closing in as Bill Downs looked up to see Danny and the Mexican mute. "By God, Danny, can't you find your way to your herd?"

Delmar joined them. "What's on your mind, Reed?"

Dismounting wearily, Danny began. He told them exactly what had happened. Staring down at his boots, he admitted that he was not the man to boss a herd. He asked for their help. Whatever the price might be, he was willing to pay it.

"If you want, I'll leave the whole damn country. I've been a fool, and so has anybody else who listened to that half-baked banker. Not one of us knew what it would be like out here. I'll say this. It separates the men from the boys."

Delmar stood with his feet apart. Bill Downs had his hand on his gun and Delmar shook his head. "Shit," Delmar said in disgust. "Danny, what do you take us for? If we take your herd in with ours, them Cheyenne will come down on me and my herd. I can't ask these men to git killed just to save the Thompson herd. Them hollerin' bastards will probably hit us anyway."

"Why don't I just shoot this son of a bitch?" Bill cut in. "He's done nothing but cause trouble from day one."

Nellie spoke up behind him. " 'Cause, Bill, he's tellin' the truth. and if I know anything about men, I mean real men, they can't leave people to die."

"Besides, there's a law agin that," Uncle Ted added. "The only decent thing to do is to help them."

Delmar held up his hand. "Hold on here. We're not goin' to fight over this. We're goin' to put it to a vote. Everyone will have a chance to say *yea* or *nay*. The way the vote goes is the way it will be. Two of us will go on one side of the herd and two on the other. We'll tell everyone and git their answers. Then we'll know."

Delmar and Bill went one way, Nellie, Uncle Ted, and Danny went the other. The mute Mexican followed Delmar and Bill. It was well past ten o'clock before they returned.

"Well, how did it come out?" Nellie asked.

"Dead even," Bill said. "And you?"

"Well, we got six to four, six *yes*, four *no*."

"Well, I'll be damned. If Delmar and I say *no*, then we won't have to help 'em, and I say *no*," Bill said flatly.

"I'll go along with Bill," Delmar said slowly. "So the *nos* have it by one vote."

"No, that's not true," Uncle Ted insisted. "You said everyone, didn't you?"

"Yes."

"Well, what about him?" Ted pointed at the mute.

"Hell, he can't talk," Bill said.

"Yeah, but he can hear." Uncle Ted motioned for the mute to come toward them. "Delmar, you explain it to him and see if he understands."

The mute was told the best way Delmar knew how. "Do you understand?" Delmar asked.

The Mexican nodded that he did. He looked across at Nellie. She winked at him and a smile came over his face.

"Well, how do you vote?"

The mute looked from one to another, then slowly nodded *yes*.

"I'll be damned!" Delmar said. He trusted the mute Mexican. More than once he had called Delmar's attention to trouble spots along the trail.

"Well, we're tied even." Delmar looked at a helpless Danny Reed. "Damned if I won't cuss myself for the rest of my life. I'll probably git lucky and git myself shot. But I can't help myself, Bill, I got to help 'em."

Delmar turned to walk away and was suddenly caught around the neck. Nellie kissed him. "You're one hell of a man!" she whispered as she let him go.

Slowly, Delmar pulled away. Over his shoulder he said, "Pass the word. We help 'em. In fact, we're takin' over their herd."

Bill shook his head. "I should of kept the Chinaman on." He chuckled. "Gee Klist, boss, do you know what you're doin'?"

Delmar had a heart, all right. Bill was not sure if it was for the Thompson crew or the cattle, but there was a difference. If he had been the boss, the Thompson crew and herd could go to hell. Then another thought came to Bill. *There are probably some good men among us. Maybe John Roper's murderer is among us to boot.* Bill was sure, if they found him, the only way he would ever make it to trial would be over Delmar's dead body. Bill had a gut feeling that before this drive was over, he would see Delmar in action.

Everyone came to life with the banging of the frying pan. They had come to hate the sound. It meant food, but it also meant morning. So far no one had gotten over four hours sleep a night. Bill swore every morning that someday he would go somewhere and sleep for a week. "No, two weeks," he muttered to himself as he pulled on his boots.

Every morning, after Bill fought his way out of his bedroll, he found Delmar calmly sipping coffee, waiting for the crew. This morning, as Bill took a plate and some coffee, Delmar said, "I want you, the mute, and another hand to go back and push the Thompson herd like all hell is after you. I'll slow down as soon as I can."

"Keep the mute close to you all the time." Bill looked up, ready to ask why. Delmar went on, "John was stabbed, and I don't want it to happen to you."

Bill nodded. "I'll walk them cows 'til their legs wear off. I don't want them screamin' redskins comin' after me."

Delmar grinned. "If they do, Bill, you fight like you never fought before. I'll have a lookout watchin' just in case. Good luck. And one more thing, take it easy on Danny Reed. He just overplayed his hand, I think. He'll be all right once he gits someone around who's been around."

Bill motioned for the mute to follow him. The mute looked at Delmar with a question in his eyes. Delmar nodded and the mute smiled. He knew that Delmar trusted him. Delmar was not sure whether he had made the right decision until Jingo rode up. Delmar told him what was going on. Jingo nodded and said, "My other friend, he will watch, too." Jingo rode out again and a few minutes later, his friend was riding with Delmar.

Delmar headed for the herd point and within an hour, he was riding alongside the point rider. The point rider was Jim McKenna, a rancher who had five hundred head in the herd. McKenna had always sworn that all bankers were crooked and that no man could trust them. Delmar secretly agreed with him.

▲▲▲

fourteen

Aside from being a little heavy around the middle, Jim McKenna was a pleasant man to be around. After a few minutes of idle conversation, Jim asked, "Well, are we goin' to take on the Thompson herd?"

"Yeah," Delmar replied. "I'll probably regret it the rest of my life, which might not be too long if those Cheyennes come hollerin' down on us."

McKenna grinned. "Won't be the first time. I fought 'em before. Just so you don't feel like a damn fool all by yourself, I voted to help the Thompson herd."

"I thought so by the way you was talkin'. "

"I took the liberty of ridin' on up ahead early this mornin'. There's a big open valley with a stream up ahead, about three miles. Good grass, be a good spot to hold up a day or so."

Delmar pulled his horse up. "Looks like you're ahead of me, Jim. That's what I came up here to find out, if there was such a place within ten miles."

McKenna said, "I'll take the herd to the north end. When the Thompson bunch gets here, they'll find fresh water and grass. I kinda think they'll need it. See you at supper."

Delmar rode back down the right flank of the herd. He was proud of his herd; they looked good. In fact, he was sure they had gained a little. A bunch of about twenty cows came toward him, drifting away from the main herd. The Mexicans quickly turned them back.

Delmar reined his horse quickly to the right just as a shot rang out, knocking his hat off. A few yards away, a horse neighed in pain. Delmar turned to see the Mexican's horse drop, rolling wild-eyed into the dust. Delmar hit the ground, rifle in hand, picking up his hat on the run. He found the Mexican pinned under the dying animal, and after several minutes they managed to free his leg. It was broken just below the knee.

His eyes full of pain, the Mexican spoke not a word. The sweat ran down both men's faces as they crouched behind the fallen horse, watching for some kind of movement, but there was none. Signaling to the Mexican, Delmar went to get his horse. The Mexican pointed to Delmar's rifle, and Delmar handed it to him. Delmar took off at a run, expecting another shot any minute.

Keeping the horse's body between him and the direction of the previous shot, somewhere to the east, Delmar returned to his injured friend. Concluding that the danger was past, he helped the Mexican into the saddle and swung up behind him. He carried the rifle while the crippled man guided the horse.

An hour later they found the chuck wagon and quickly went to work on the broken leg. Within twenty minutes the leg was set and the Mexican rested in the wagon with a half bottle of whiskey.

The supply wagon arrived with Nellie and Uncle Ted. Looking at Delmar's hat, Uncle Ted whistled. "Kinda close."

"Yeah," Delmar answered. "A hard way to get a haircut."

Taking charge, Nellie rolled up the extra bandages, and helped transfer the man to the supply wagon where she could take care of him.

"I'll see you all later," Delmar said. "I want to take a look around."

Nellie started to protest, but swallowed her words.

Delmar swung into the saddle and was gone.

As she watched him ride away, she felt empty. She was always watching him ride away.

▲▲▲

fifteen

Bill Downs could not believe his eyes. There were cattle scattered from hell to breakfast. Randy Shummer rode with him. Shummer was only twenty-four, a double-barreled hell-raiser and a hard worker. From a good family, he was tall, lean, and quick with his hands. He had worked for John Roper for two years and Bill liked him. He and Randy had shared many a drink together.

The mute looked the situation over. He made a sign that the cattle were spread out too far and smiled.

Bill nodded. "You're sure right there, Mex, my boy."

Danny Reed rode out to meet them. "We been roundin' up cattle, tryin' to get 'em into some kind of formation."

Bill said, "Well, Delmar wants 'em pushed north right away. He said he'd have a lookout posted somewhere. Randy, you go down that right flank and turn them cattle north and start 'em walkin'. Danny, you git two of your best men and start pushin' them drags as hard as God will let you. If you can, push 'em right through the herd. Come on, Mex, we'll take the left flank. Let's move cattle, men, daylight's burnin'!"

The first thing Bill noticed was the shape the cattle were in. He did not like what he saw. They needed a two-week rest on good feed. Then it would still be a question as to whether they were fit to trail. Bill muttered, "Damn poor management." But he was satisfied things were soon going to change.

The first two riders they met were not happy about the takeover and told Bill so. "We don't give a damn what you say, we work for Danny Reed."

"Is that so?" he asked.

"Yeah, that's so," the tall, hard-looking one on the right concluded.

"Well, gentlemen, I want you to split up and drive cows, not wander around and bullshit each other. You're on a cattle drive, not a picnic."

"You're an insulting son of a bitch. What we should do is teach you a lesson on how we run things here."

Bill looked at the mute. "Well, why don't you bigmouth assholes try?"

The one closest to Bill started for his gun, but the mute had him covered before he had it half-drawn. Bill rode forward and relieved them of their weapons. "Now, you muscle-brained bastards, git down and walk."

The men dismounted and Bill took their horses. The mute just sat smiling. He and Bill rode away, leaving them standing. The next drovers they met were considerably quicker to start the cattle moving.

Bill turned the horses over to Danny. He measured his words carefully, "Any man who won't work for me and do as I say don't eat or ride."

Danny agreed. "Bill's the boss, so you all better get pushin' cows or walk hungry."

Bill gave the grizzled old cook his orders, "If you feed one of those lazy bastards, you'll be boilin' biscuits in hell, understand?"

The old cook gave his word, "They won't eat at this wagon. We been needin' a boss for a long time."

"Well, now you got one," Bill said. "I came back here to help you get to Kansas, not git killed by Indians."

Randy Shummer made it to camp just before dark. He looked like he had been whipped over the head with a wet sack. With skinned knuckles and a black eye, he was not in a good mood.

"What happened to you?" Bill asked.

"Well, there's a couple of bastards who won't be chewin' too good for a few days. I told 'em what you said and they got real owly about it, so I kicked their asses and got their names. The rest is up to you."

Bill smiled. "You're a pretty good ramrod."

Randy managed a battered grin. "Well, the right flank is goin' north and if the left flank can keep up, we just might git a drive goin'. "

The mute tapped Randy on the shoulder. Pulling some salve from his saddlebag, he handed it to Randy, motioning that he should put it on.

"That stuff is all right," Randy said. "You should've been a doctor."

The Mexican nodded, pointing to himself, indicating that he was.

"Do you believe this guy?" Randy asked Bill.

"Well, I don't know if he's as good with medicine as he is with that gun. Maybe he can cure hoof-and-mouth and shippin' fever."

The next two days were pure hell on man and beast. There were more cuss words and impudent remarks let fly than could be found in the world record books. Bill Downs was so tired, he staggered when he walked. The only good thing about it was that by the end of the third day, they could see the Roper herd twelve miles to the north. In another half day's drive, the two herds would become one.

There was no sign of Indians, no smoke, no tracks, no nothing, but Bill never let up. "Let's go!" he yelled. "We'll be caught up by noon."

The eastern sky was still flushed with pink. The men moved slowly, spoke little, and tempers were short. The two men who had walked for half a day decided they would work for Bill. The two drovers Shummer had fought with were healing up nicely. They worked willingly with the rest, no complaints. Randy Shummer proved he could handle men as well as cattle. He was everywhere on the right flank. It was just as he had said, the left flank had a hard time keeping up without causing the cattle to mill in a big circle.

The Roper crew helped them the last two miles, and Delmar rode out to meet Bill. "Well, you made it this far," Delmar said, eyeing him. "But you look like you haven't slept in a week."

"I ain't," Bill answered. "The cattle need rest and feed, mainly feed. But I'm sure you can see that. We'll let 'em rest up a couple of days and fill up."

"The range is good up ahead, plenty of water," Delmar said. "Did you see any Indians?"

"No, not one."

Delmar shook his head. "That could mean something."

"It could," Bill agreed.

"You go to camp. You and the mute git some sleep. I'll send the rest of your crew in as soon as I can git these cattle to yonder valley. They'll mix with ours by mornin'. "

Bill waved for the mute to follow him, but the mute shook his head and pointed to Delmar. Grinning, Bill waved and said, "Okay, Mex. See you later." He rode away with nothing but sleep on his mind.

As they rode around the herd, Delmar checked his horse and reined closer to the mute. "He's quite a man," he said, pointing toward Bill as he receded in the distance.

The mute smiled and held up one finger.

Delmar grinned, "Yeah, he's one of a kind, all right. Did he work you hard?"

The mute nodded *yes,* making a sign that encircled the entire herd.

"You mean he worked everybody hard?"

A smile was his answer.

"Did he have any trouble?"

The mute patted his gun.

"You took care of it?"

Again a smile.

"Did you shoot anybody?"

The mute shook his head.

"That's good," Delmar said.

The mute pointed to the hole in Delmar's hat.

"Yeah, someone shot at me. Killed your buddy's horse. It fell on him and broke his leg."

The mute frowned and patted his gun again.

Delmar laughed. "You don't think it would have happened if you were there?"

The mute smiled again.

Delmar offered tobacco and they both rolled a smoke. As Delmar sat watching the herd pass by, the mute signaled for him to return to camp.

"Why?" Delmar asked.

The mute made signs of sleep.

"Okay, let's go then. You want me to go to camp so you can sleep."

Besides catching up on lost sleep, the Thompson crew spent the next two days getting acquainted with the Roper crew. Since some preferred to use their knuckles, the mute was kept busy breaking up fights with his riata. Lassoing one or both men, he would jerk them to the ground, then smile and pat his gun. He soon got the nickname, Patty Gun.

No one ever challenged him. It was common knowledge that no one could handle a gun like he did. Every evening he spent countless hours practicing. He could run, throw himself to the ground, turn a somersault, and come up shooting. Some claimed he could outdraw Wesley Hardin or Crazy Bill Anderson.

On the evening of the third day, Delmar announced, "We start north in the mornin'. You pokes git as much rest as you can, daylight comes early." He walked over to where Bill Downs, Jingo, Randy Shummer, and a few others were drinking coffee. "Let's go relieve the guard, Bill. Shummer, you and Jingo might as well come along."

Delmar felt uneasy as the four rode out around the herd. The moon rose slowly, a golden glow on the dark horizon. Jingo dropped back, and the others rode on. A coyote yelped, answered by another, then another and another. As another coyote howled Bill and Delmar froze. Delmar slowly reached for his rifle and Bill followed his example.

Delmar's mind raced as coyotes howled all around them. He knew in an instant that they were in trouble.

▲▲▲

sixteen

They were too far from camp to warn anyone. "I doubt if they could hear a rifle shot this far away," Delmar said.

"Shit," Bill whispered. "I knew it was too good to be true. What the hell are they doin' out here in the dark?"

Delmar did not answer the question. "We could make a run for it. Somehow we got to git back to camp."

"I'll go," Bill suggested.

"No, we'll both go. We'll ride back the way we came, slow and easy. If they jump us, then we'll ride like hell."

They turned their horses and headed back. They had gone some fifty yards when a dark shadow came from out of nowhere, trying to pull Bill from his horse. Without a second thought, Delmar turned and clubbed the Indian over the head with his rifle butt. Bill pulled his six-gun and put two shots in the still form. Suddenly there were dark forms all around them. Firing at anything that moved, they spurred their horses into a dead run toward camp.

The camp was in chaos, full of shouting and gunfire. Cattle were running everywhere and men were doing the same. Uncle Ted was firing from under the supply wagon. Delmar could only hope Nellie was safe. Random gunfire flashed in the darkness. Then, as suddenly as it began, the Indian attack stopped.

As the drovers gathered together, Delmar said, "We'll just sit tight 'til daylight. Then we can see what damage has been done."

"I know one thing," one drover said, "I ain't leavin' this camp 'til I can see! I woke up and went to take a piss and a damn Injun jumped me. I got him off me, but now I need to change clothes."

As the mute pulled on Delmar's sleeve, Delmar turned toward him and asked, "What is it?"

The mute went to Delmar's horse, pointed and made signs indicating other horses.

"All of them?" Delmar shouted.

The mute held up two fingers.

"Oh, shit, you mean we're all afoot?"

The mute nodded.

"Oh, my God, Bill!" Delmar shouted.

Bill Downs came on the run. "What is it?" he asked, gun in hand.

"Bill, my good man, we're afoot. Yes, damn it! Can't you hear? Them dirty Injun bastards stole our horses."

"Hell, I got mine and you got yours."

"Damn it, man, thirty men can't ride two horses!"

Bill was sure he was going to be sick, There were only four horses in camp. The team that pulled the chuck wagon and two saddle horses.

"Where's Jingo and Shummer?"

No one knew.

"Well, I'll go and find out," Bill said.

It was still dark as he rode out. Then, as the sun rose, Bill found Jingo's body, lying scalped in a pool of blood. From the look of the ground, he had put up one hell of a fight.

Bill dreaded looking for Shummer. He found Shummer's dead horse, but no trace of its rider. As dawn broke over the valley, the cattle grazed quietly as if nothing had happened. Bill circled the herd, then returned to camp.

As Bill arrived, Shummer stood waiting, "Some fight, eh boss?"

"Yeah, what happened to your horse?"

"I was knocked off and came up shootin'. They tried to steal my horse, but I shot him and got a couple of Injuns to boot."

"Well, Randy, you just became a shepherd."

"Yeah, I heard," Randy replied. "I never drove cows on foot before."

"You better get used to it."

As Danny Reed approached, Bill Downs snarled. "You know I just want to whip your ass. Damn you, why don't you just go someplace and die?"

Danny sighed. "I wish I could, but somehow I just don't have the guts to shoot myself." Shrugging his shoulders, he walked away alone.

Delmar sat absently scratching with a stick in the dirt. He turned to Bill and said, "We got more trouble."

"Like what?" Bill could not imagine anything worse than what had already happened.

"The Mex with the broken leg is out of his head with fever. His leg turned black and it don't look good for him."

"Blood poison?" Bill asked.

"Yeah, that's the way it looks. According to the cook, the only way to save him is to cut it off. Then he still might die."

"Who's goin' to cut it off?" Bill asked.

"I thought maybe..."

Bill backed away. "Not me Delmar. Hell, no. He'd die sure as hell. Besides, I'm no good with a knife. Now and then I cut a piece of meat to fry, but if I ain't careful I'll cut myself."

"Well, do you know of anybody who could cut it off? The cook won't."

"Yeah, by God, I do."

Delmar stood up. "Who?"

"The Mex."

"You mean the mute?"

"Yeah, he told us he was some kind of doctor."

"I'll be damned," Delmar said. "Go fetch him."

The mute climbed out of the supply wagon and shook his head.

"Real bad?" Bill asked.

The mute nodded.

"Can you save him?"

The mute threw up his hands.

"Will you try?"

The mute nodded that he would.

"Do you need help?"

The mute pointed toward the cook.

Bill walked away. There was nothing more he could do. It was up to God and the mute Mexican. Delmar stalked around camp, saying nothing. No one spoke to him, well aware that he wanted to be left alone.

Seven thousand cows and no horses, fifteen days by horseback from help of any kind. Things were not going according to plan. And to top everything off, there was no guarantee the Indians would not raid them again.

Delmar stared at the spot where the horses had been tethered. Saddles and riding gear were scattered everywhere. He kicked a saddle out of his way. *Damn the luck anyway. There is no way we can do a damn thing on foot.*

A big rangy steer spooked at Delmar's approach. From his new perspective, on foot, Delmar noticed the size of the steers feeding around him. He considered that he had only one team to pull the chuck wagon, and none to pull the supply wagons. He could get by with one chuck wagon, but supply wagons for both herds were a necessity. He turned toward camp, some fifty yards away.

The camp waited in silence for word from the supply wagon. All eyes fastened on Delmar as he returned to camp and helped himself to a cup of coffee. *What the hell do they expect of me? I'm not God. Only God can perform miracles.* He was not sure he could even muster up enough good words to bury somebody.

Hell, he thought, *I'm nothing but the town drunk and right now I'd git damn drunk if I could!* But he was quite sure the crippled Mexican had drunk up most of the whiskey. *Besides, he needs it a lot more than I do, poor bastard.* As Delmar looked at the sun, he guessed it was a little past two o'clock.

The mute came out of the supply wagon carrying the leg of his friend. Most of the crew turned away, a few left the camp retching. The mute made a sign that he wanted a shovel to bury it. Delmar helped him dig the hole.

There was no use saying anything about it. If the man lived, which Delmar doubted, it would prove one thing: the mute was a doctor. *But how the hell does a mute become a doctor?* The question turned over and over in Delmar's mind. Maybe they taught him in Mexico.

The mute put the shovel away and drank a cup of coffee as if nothing had happened.

"He sure is a cool son of a bitch!" Bill admitted. "I guess I expected him to be more concerned."

"He probably is. He just don't show it."

The mute smiled at Delmar, threw the cold coffee from his cup, pointed to the herd and then toward the north.

Irritated, Delmar said, "You know we don't have any horses."

The mute grabbed Delmar's arm, nodding his head. Everyone in the camp, some thirty men, stared at the mute Mexican as if he were crazy."

"I don't understand," Delmar said, pulling away.

The mute signaled desperately, trying to make Delmar understand.

Delmar shook his head. "Show me, my friend, then I'll understand."

The mute smiled. He went to one of the horses and mounted up, motioning for Delmar to watch. Holding his riata, he rode toward a big steer, the same one Delmar had noticed. He swung the rope high over his head, then jerked the beast down. As Delmar ran to help him, the other drovers came running. Puzzled, Delmar and half a dozen others held the steer down while the Mexican picked out a saddle and bridle from the scattered riding gear.

Suddenly, Delmar got the idea. "By God, Bill, we can do it!"

All Bill Downs could do was blink in astonishment. "If we can, boss man, I'll marry this mute and shoot my mother-in-law. So help me I'll damn sure give it one hell of a try!"

"No, Bill, you got it only half right. We're goin' to do it. We're goin' to break every damn steer in this herd to ride if we have to, and we'll do most of it on the trail."

Within a matter of minutes, the brute was saddled and bridled. The mute stepped forward, smiling. He mounted the beast and signaled for it to be turned loose. They let go and stepped back as hooves began to fly. Mingled shouts, laughter, and curses filled the air.

The steer bucked, bawled, and ran in a circle, but the mute rode like he was born to it. Within twenty minutes the big steer played out, stopping dead in its tracks. Everyone expected the mute to step down. Instead, he waved them back and waited. After a short rest, the steer tried running again. Finally, after several hours, the animal moved only when kicked in the ribs and stopped when commanded to do so.

The mute motioned that they bring a rope. He tied it around the steer's horns and then stepped down as a half dozen men held the beast. Tying the other end of the rope to the saddle horn, the mute mounted his horse and pulled the reluctant steer to the supply wagon.

At daylight, the mute saddled the steer and went for a ride. Bellowing in protest, at first the steer resisted, but then it began to get the message: when those big Mexican spurs raked its ribs, it was time to move, and in the right direction. By evening of the second day, the steer was working reasonably well, enough to convince Delmar and Bill that they had found the way north.

Nellie and Uncle Ted had been kept busy nursing the one-legged Mexican, but they took time out to watch the mute doctor, as Uncle Ted called him, ride the big steer.

"You know, Nellie, we got saddle cows instead of saddle horses."

Nellie laughed. "We'll be known from now on as the cow riders."

Ted grinned. "I can't wait to see the look on the faces in Dodge when they see this outfit come trailin' in. They won't believe it 'til they see it. Wait 'til tomorrow when they really start breakin' them steers!"

"It'll be one hell of a show!" Nellie agreed.

The following day, the mute roped ten steers to be broken. By four o'clock some had ridden their new mounts a mile or more, while others were still trying to climb into the saddle.

As Randy Shummer described it, there were cattle scattered all over hell and half a foreign country.

▲▲▲

seventeen

No one seemed worried about the herd. Worry accomplished nothing without saddle stock. After several days, the mute, at least, had something to ride. Besides breaking the steer, the mute began feeding the animal corn with salt on it. The salt-hungry animal could not resist, and Delmar became convinced that corn would keep the animal in good shape as it carried the added weight of a rider.

Uncle Ted, who claimed he knew how to build an ox yoke, bustled about his task. The mute chose several big steers for the teams and began the formidable chore of breaking them to work. First he tied them hard and fast to the back of the wagon, hooked up the team and spent hours driving them around. The second day he made a complete circuit of the herd. The third day he put Uncle Ted's makeshift yoke on them and led them some more. The following day, leaving his one-legged friend and Nellie behind, he hooked the cattle to the supply wagon and went around the herd again. After being led a few more days, the cattle would be ready.

The men breaking steers had managed to break a half-dozen and were ready to start north. Delmar told the men to ride only half a day per steer, and if they rode hard, only two hours.

"We'll need half the herd!" Shummer declared.

"I don't care if we have to break every one of 'em. We're goin' north in the mornin', so get used to the idea. We won't make six or eight miles a day, but we will make four. I don't care if you have to break steers all night and drive cows in your sleep, I want two new steers broke to lead behind the wagons every mornin'. Change 'em at noon every day, and I mean every day, from now on, 'til we see how these critters are goin' to hold up. We're not out to kill our saddle stock."

The morning brought a show that belonged in the circus. It was past ten before the herd took on any kind of shape, but then it began moving north.

"Thank God this stream runs north and south," Bill Downs said. "We'll be on good feed for a week anyway. I never rode anything so damn rough in my life."

"Me neither," Shummer agreed. "My ass feels like I been used for a snubbing post in a rough string corral."

"At least we ain't walkin', " Bill replied.

"I do once in a while," Shummer admitted. "Every chance I git."

Bill smiled. "So do I."

Nellie and Uncle Ted were thankful they could ride in the wagon. They had another reason to be thankful: their patient was doing better every day. The only thing not up to par was their speed. The herd moved at a crawl, like a giant snake, but every step north meant progress.

Smiling as he always did when he was pleased, the Mexican gave his steer to Delmar. Holding up one finger, Delmar grinned: this steer was one of a kind. The mute nodded and again he proved to be right. The big brindle steer could take a half-day's ride with no trouble.

Delmar noticed that about one out of five steers made good saddle stock, and after only two weeks on the trail, each drover had broken a string of good steers. Their speed was almost up to what they could do with horses. No one would believe it, but it was happening.

The men were in good spirits. After Bill caught some of them racing their steers, Delmar raised hell, but down deep he wished he had seen it. The talk around camp was that Danny Reed had the fastest steer in the whole herd. But Delmar had the only steer that would work a rope, thanks to the mute.

"I wonder what that damn banker would say if he could see this outfit now?" Bill Downs asked one afternoon.

Delmar laughed. "I don't know, he'd probably dirty his pants."

"I wonder if these so-called saddle steers can swim?"

"Damned if I know, but I got a feeling we're about to find out," Delmar said. "We got us a river crossin' comin' up."

"I'll admit I need a bath, boss, but that'll be a long wet one."

Delmar continued. "The point rider said we'll be crossin' the Canadian about noon tomorrow. All the other rivers we've crossed is just streams compared to this one. After we cross it we got a dry drive, very little water 'til we hit the Palo Duro. We follow it 'til it stops in Oklahoma. Just where, only God knows."

"So the big swim is tomorrow," Bill said.

"Maybe we'll stay on this side 'til the next mornin', then cross while everything is fresh."

Bill smiled. "I'd hate to drown tired." Kicking his big spotted steer into a trot, he left Delmar to his thoughts.

▲▲▲

eighteen

The powerful brindle steer plodded along, carrying the trail boss to the crossing a little after two o'clock in the afternoon.

Delmar passed the word: they would cross the following day. Each drover was to get his best mount ready.

The rest of the day was spent putting tail ropes on their saddles so they wouldn't slip over the steers' heads when they went downhill. The mute showed them how when they were breaking the steers to ride. Without the tail ropes, the saddles worked forward and sooner or later would slide over the steers' heads. The cowboys had learned another valuable lesson: they had to shorten their stirrups. If they didn't, most of the cowboys' legs were so long their feet barely cleared the ground, and riding in river brush was hard on feet and legs.

Some looked like English jockeys. But most took up their stirrups a couple of notches. "My prize steer, Old Slut," Randy Shummer responded, "is gettin' a little footsore, but he will make the crossin'. Then I can turn him loose. He won't leave me anyway. He knows where the corn and salt comes from. I got plenty more."

"I got Big Spot and he ain't bad." Bill Downs sipped hot coffee.

"That Big Spot probably can't swim a damn lick." Bill agreed.

"What about Big Law?" Randy asked.

"I don't know," Bill commented. "He seems to be all right." "What about that brindle you ride, boss? Can he swim?"

Delmar looked up. "You mean my cow?"

"Yes, I mean your cow, whatever you call him."

"Well, me and my cow done had us a talk. He don't drown me and I won't kill him. I took him by the cook wagon a while ago so he'd get the idea. Boiled beef and beans or become half duck."

So that they would float high in the water, Bill and some of the men tied big logs to both sides of the wagons.

Nellie was excited. "Do we cross first or last?" she asked Uncle Ted.

"We cross first. If we git the chow on the other side, them cowboys will come across when they git hungry."

"Seems to me they're always hungry," Nellie said, a faraway look in her eyes. She was looking at the river. It was so wide, so beautiful, surrounded by cool grass and trees. As soon as it was dark she would go for a swim.

Most of the crew had already ridden up river to cool off and take a much-needed bath. Some rode their saddle steers, which had every name from Whore-Chaser to Snake Bite. One called his Dreamer, another Big Dummy. Danny Reed's steer was Dollar Wide. but the one who got the most attention was Shummer's Old Slut. Old Slut never wandered very far from camp. He loved corn and was crazy after salt.

The hardworking cattle pulling the wagon had become pets. Nellie named them Butch and Dutch. Sometimes, however, in difficult circumstances, Uncle Ted neglected to call them that. One of Bill Downs's steers, Loco, was a candidate to pull the wagon if anything happened to Butch or Dutch. Loco was a huge, gentle beast, probably the largest steer in the whole bunch. Delmar and Bill decided to tie him to the back of the wagon, to use him as a Judas goat, hoping the rest, crowded at the point of the herd, would follow him into the water.

The wagon made slow progress crossing the river. Nellie became convinced the Canadian was a mile wide, but Uncle Ted assured her it was only an eighth of a mile. Loco, tied behind the wagon, served the purpose, getting the rest of the herd started. But the cattle pulling the wagon were slow swimmers, drifting further downstream than anyone had anticipated. When they finally came to the opposite bank, it was too steep for them to pull the wagon up. The cook quickly unhitched his team and came to their rescue.

Frightened, Nellie almost jumped out of the wagon into the river, but Randy Shummer persuaded her that the river was infested with snakes.

"What did you tell her that for?" Bill Downs asked. "Hell, there ain't no snakes in this river that would hurt anybody!"

Randy smiled. "I know that, but she stayed in the wagon, didn't she?"

"Oh, yeah, she stayed all right. Did you know she went swimming last night?"

Randy looked surprised. "No, I didn't, but I'll bet she won't do it again." He kicked Slut in the ribs. "Come on, Slut, Let's go. We better point them relations of yours in the right direction. Wouldn't want your cousins to get lost."

Slut refused to move, and Randy was about to get his attention when he saw Bill Downs running across the backs of the swimming cattle, trying to reach the center. Midstream, the cattle had started to mill in a tight circle. Bill dropped down on a big red steer, spurring like a madman. The steer let out a bawl and threw his body half out of the water. Without letting up, Bill kept spurring, and through brute strength, the terrified animal broke free, literally pushing some twenty cattle ahead of him. The milling cattle followed, swimming toward the far shore.

"God Almighty!" Randy muttered under his breath. One misstep on Bill's part could have meant certain death.

As the milling cattle made their way to the shore, Randy and the other drovers heaved a sigh of relief, then a shout went up from both banks of the river. But Bill could not hear the shouting; he was too busy swimming to shore. Little did he know the respect he had just gained.

Delmar rode to meet him. "That was a damn fool thing to do. You know that, don't you? But I guess it did work," he said dryly.

Dripping, Bill grinned. "Hell, boss, Shummer said there were snakes in that river!"

Delmar shook his head. "Snakes, my ass, you're as crazy as Shummer." He rode away with a good feeling. There was no doubt about it: Bill Downs had saved many a cow from drowning and a lot of hours to boot.

A dozen or more cattle were stuck in the quicksand, but the chuckwagon team and a couple of good ropes soon had them out. Shortly after noon, the river crossing was made. The cattle would spend the rest of the day grazing and the crew would get a chance to dry out. The saddle stock could swim all right, but not with men on their backs.

The next morning, they left the Canadian River for the long hot drive to the Palo Duro River, hoping to find water somewhere in between.

▲▲▲

nineteen

From his hilltop vantage point, Randy Shummer watched the dust cloud that hung over the slow-moving herd. He had put some hard miles on his old saddle steer, but Slut was still eager to work. Water was what they were looking for, but so far, nothing. He ran a hand across his whiskered jaw. Straining his eyes once again toward the north, he searched for some sign of green grass and trees, anything that grew where water was. His eyes burned from the strain. He squeezed them shut, only to feel them fill with tears as he opened them again. He must go and report to Delmar: no water in sight, another dry camp.

He rolled a smoke, slipping the Bull Durham pouch back in his shirt pocket. Old Slut stood patiently waiting. *What a hell of a way to live,* he thought. Then he spoke to the steer as he mounted. "Shit, I'd rather git whipped with a bullwhip than go tell 'em no water. We either got too much or not enough."

There was no need for Randy to say a word as he rode into camp. Everyone knew.

"How long can we keep this up?" Danny Reed asked. "Anyone care to answer?"

No one did. If anyone had known, he would have spoken up long before. The grass crunched underfoot, burned beyond ever becoming green again.

"We can't drive these cattle tomorrow in this heat," Delmar spoke from cracked lips. "We'll drive all night, soon as the moon comes up. We might lose a few in the dark, but it's better to lose a few than all of 'em."

The mute Mexican grinned and nodded his head. And if the mute agreed, everyone else did, too. So far he had never been wrong, and every one of the drovers respected his good judgment. Everyone liked him. He had probably helped every one of them in some small way. After all, he was the best shot, the best rider, and beyond a doubt, the best steer rider in the bunch.

Although they had never seen Delmar pull a gun, most of the men had heard Roper say he was the best. So there was talk among them of a contest between Delmar and the mute.

"I think the mute would win," Danny Reed suggested more than once.

Bill Downs chuckled. "I don't think you could git Delmar to pull a gun unless he was forced to—but then he'd break loose."

"There's no doubt about it," Randy Shummer agreed. "He'd be hard to stop. I wouldn't even want to try."

Driving the herd at night proved to be the answer. They made faster time and even the cattle seemed to sense they had to make time and distance. By ten o'clock, the sun again scorched the earth, and the drovers were signaled to stop pushing. They let the cattle spread out, grazing on whatever they could find. Some of the trail-broken steers kept moving north, grabbing a mouthful of brown grass here and there, eating on the move without anyone to slow them down. They would be strung out for miles, but as Delmar put it, "We won't have to drive 'em if they go by themselves. We'll push the drags tonight."

Three days without water had taken their toll. They had already started to lose cattle, and some were just too weak to go on. They would surely die. Little was said, but the drovers were becoming edgy. Their eyes were red from lack of sleep, and some stumbled when they walked.

"We got to find water soon," Delmar said to Bill. "These men are as bad off as the cattle."

It was the mute who first realized that the leaders had found water. At two o'clock in the morning, the cattle began moving faster and he pointed it out to Delmar. At four o'clock, the point rider, a short, fat rider named Bouden, brought a report. He was grinning from ear to ear. "Water ahead, boss!"

Delmar nodded. "Tell the chuckwagon to speed it up a bit. You show 'em the way."

It proved to be a small stream, no more than three feet wide and four inches deep with good grass along the banks. It ran from the northeast as far as the eye could see. It was daylight, and with no way to control the cattle, Delmar turned to the mute and said, "Pass the word, we rest here."

He rode toward the chuck wagon. As he dismounted, Nellie poured him a cup of coffee. "A rough stretch, Del, but we made it," she said.

Delmar tried to grin, but his mouth was too sore. "Yeah, we're this far. I wonder how far it is to the Palo Duro River?"

Uncle Ted scratched his head. "Damned if I know, but it can't be far."

"This might not be a river," Bill Downs said as he joined them, "But I'll settle for it any day." It was the sweetest stream this side of heaven.

As the herd followed the stream to the northeast, it became larger. Even so, gaunt and tired, the cattle still suffered from the earlier lack of water. But the loss was far less than Delmar expected. The drive without water had cost them over two hundred head. After guessing over five hundred, Delmar was glad to discover his error.

The saddle steers were holding up amazingly well. The crew was sure they had just driven a herd of cattle through hell itself. According to Danny Reed, the only difference between hell and a dry drive was that the sun did not shine in hell while it shone all the time in Texas.

Bill Downs's records showed they had been on the trail some forty days, and by Uncle Ted's reckoning they were over halfway. Somehow no one was excited about only being halfway.

The herd was moving well. The sun had yet to reach its zenith when the drovers saw a group of riders outlined against the sky.

The mute rode up and tugged at Delmar's sleeve.

"I see 'em," Delmar said slowly, "What do you make of it?"

The mute patted his gun.

Delmar nodded in agreement. "Do you think they'll try to take the herd?"

The mute shook his head. He rubbed his fingers together.

"Money?" Delmar asked.

The mute smiled.

Delmar had heard about such operations. A gang of outlaws would demand money to cross their territory, or territory they claimed. If payment was not forthcoming, the shoot-out was on. Delmar hoped to God this was not the case, but the mute had yet to be proved wrong.

Bill Downs showed up on his big spotted steer, and far across the herd, Randy Shummer, Danny Reed, and three other riders began making their way toward them. Everywhere Delmar looked, his men were moving toward him. A feeling of confidence came over him. He stopped the buckskin steer and motioned for his men to form a half-circle some hundred feet across. There they waited.

A grimy, black-whiskered man of about forty led a group of nearly twenty men. Approaching cautiously, they could not believe their eyes. The drovers were riding steers, not horses. "Who's in charge here?" he demanded, when he was close enough to be heard.

No one spoke.

They moved closer and his powerful voice rang out again, "By God, I asked a question! Who runs this show anyway?"

Delmar rode forward, "I do, Bigmouth. Who the hell wants to know?"

"By God, I do. You're trespassing and we won't stand for that without payment. In fact, you've been trespassing ever since you crossed the state line. By the size of your herd, we think a dollar a head will be enough to pay for the grass and water."

"And if we don't pay?" Delmar asked.

A fish-eyed *hombre,* considerably younger, started to draw his gun, but Del's gun spoke first. The outlaw toppled from his horse, a jagged hole in his throat. One after another, they went down. The mute's guns were bucking in his hands. The burly leader swayed in the saddle as the Mexican's bullets tore through his chest. As their comrades lay bleeding in the dust, only four managed to escape the spray of lead, spurring their mounts relentlessly until they were out of range.

Delmar's crew began catching horses. There were not enough to go around, but it would help save their steers and their pride.

The mute stood motionless, watching Delmar with surprise in his eyes. He shook his head and smiled. He had seen many a gun drawn, but nothing like Delmar's speed and accuracy. *Thank God I did not try to outdraw him,* he thought. *Why did Jingo lie? He knew the speed of Delmar's draw. And why did Jingo insist that he would kill both John Roper and Delmar himself?*

The mute smiled. So far he was Delmar's friend, and he intended to stay that way. Never in his life had he met such a man. He, Manuel Diego, had come from a fine family. He had studied medicine in Mexico City. But just before he was to complete his training, he spoke out against President Hernandez. He was imprisoned, tortured. They could destroy his voice, but not his mind. In the United States he was known only as a mute and an outlaw. But somehow he felt secure with Delmar. Though deadly, Delmar was an honest man.

There would be no end to what this man could do in Mexico. Manuel the mute would get an army to follow him. Manuel Diego swore to the Blessed Virgin he would be Delmar's friend for life. He wondered if Delmar could read Spanish. Somehow they would communicate and maybe someday, head to Mexico. No longer would he have to fear the president and his army. They would have an army of their own and Delmar would be the general. That night he would stop by the supply wagon to tell his friend Pancho.

As soon as the outlaws were given a proper burial, Delmar took a quick inventory of the horseflesh. Three had been wounded by stray bullets and had to be shot. One would be ready to ride in about a week. That left fourteen good horses. Delmar found himself wishing someone else would try to collect. He had gained fourteen horses and not lost a man.

"Let's go north," he told Bill Downs. "Enough of this for one day."

"We might have some more company tomorrow," Bill commented. "Them four *hombres* might go get some help."

"I don't think so," Delmar replied. "I looked that big-whiskered fella over when we laid him in the ground. I know him."

"I'll be damned! From where?" Bill asked.

"Crazy Bill Anderson's bunch. I don't know his real name, but they called him Buzzy. He was a newcomer when I was there. They didn't think too highly of him then. Crazy Bill once told me Buzzy was like a young robin, all mouth and ass. The rest didn't matter."

"It sure as hell don't matter now," Bill said. "That mute put four holes in him before he could think."

"Yeah, " Delmar replied. "But I think one would have been sufficient."

Bill gathered up the reins of his newfound horse. "Well, see you later." Bill rode off to catch up with the herd.

Some of the rest turned their steers loose to ride horses for a change. The day passed without further incident and the evening meal was eaten in silence except for an occasional word here and there. Even the mute withheld his customary smile. Nellie made a brief appearance to eat, then disappeared into the wagon to check on the one-legged Mexican. Uncle Ted sat quietly drinking his coffee. The fire flickered as a gust of wind blew in from the north. There was definitely going to be a change in the weather.

The drovers rolled up in their blankets like small mounds scattered on the Oklahoma plateau. But they came awake with a start when a clap of thunder sent them scrambling for their slickers. The rain fell in a torrent. Fiery forks of lightning zigzagged across the sky.

"All out!" came Delmar's order. "The cattle won't like this! Hold 'em in. The herd will try to drift off on us if we don't keep 'em pushed back!"

The men, alternately cussing the rain, the wind, or their saddle stock, rode out into the night with Delmar in the lead. Delmar found Randy Shummer, one of the night guards, on the far side of the herd.

"I seen it, boss, but I don't believe it!"

"What?" Del asked.

"I've heard tell of St. Elmo's fire. Well, I seen it."

"Where?"

"On them cattle," Randy replied. "Little balls of fire jumpin' all over the place, from one cow's horn to another."

"Like that?"

Randy turned in his saddle. "Yeah, like that." a small ball of fire ran from one animal to another. When the lightning flashed, the whole herd took on a pale blue cast.

"I sure hope nobody makes any unnecessary noise," Delmar said as an afterthought. "Them cows will stampede sure as hell. Damn,

I wish it was daylight. You go git some coffee and some sleep if you can. We'll keep an eye on 'em 'til mornin'."

"First it's so damn dry the brush follows the coyote around, then it rains so hard it'd wash the beans off your plate," Randy complained. "I'll see you come daylight." Randy rode away toward camp.

Delmar agreed with Randy. Every dry wash and gully would be running, bank full of muddy water for the next two or three days. The rain did not stop until late the next evening. Water stood in pools everywhere.

It was slow going, too slow to suit Delmar, with the herd moving four miles a day at best. But the cattle looked better, thriving on the cool nights. Even the days seemed cooler.

The next day, the Palo Duro River rose from out of nowhere, nearly overflowing its banks.

"Sure glad we don't have to cross that," Bill said. "Look at that rollin' mud; it'd drown any cow or horse that tried it."

"After I seen you walk on them cow's backs on the Canadian, I'd think you could walk right across and not git wet," Randy said.

Bill looked sideways at Randy. "I might be crazy, but I ain't stupid."

The mute pointed upstream. A dead horse came floating by, still wearing a saddle. The mute undid his rope. At that moment, the same thought crossed all their minds. Someone had lost his life in that slimy sea of rolling mud they called a river. The mute sat quietly watching and waiting. Suddenly his arm swung up over his head and his riata shot out into the river. He turned his horse, pulling a body from the boiling water and mud. The men gathered around the body of a blonde girl no more than eighteen or twenty.

"What do you make of it?" Randy asked.

The mute crossed himself.

"I don't know," Bill replied. "We'd better tell Delmar."

The mute agreed. He removed the rope and rode to find the trail boss.

In a matter of minutes Delmar stood looking down at the lifeless body. "What a hell of a waste," he said as he stooped down and rolled the body over. He gently removed a chain which hung around her neck. On the end of the chain was a silver cross with a green stone in the center. Delmar put it in his shirt pocket.

"Only one thing bothers me," Bill Downs said. "Where the hell did she come from? I don't remember any settlement around here. She must have come from a wagon train."

"Could be," Randy admitted.

"Well, if you fellas see anyone around lookin' for her, tell 'em I got her cross. Pick out a nice place to bury her," Del spoke over his shoulder as he mounted up. The mute followed him.

Three days up the Palo Duro, the water cleared and was dropping fast. Del began to wonder if there would be enough water for the cattle. He stopped his horse to study the tracks of several wagons. The cattle had obliterated most signs of the crossing, but on the north side of the herd the tracks were undisturbed. They were only a few hours old, and even though he could see for miles, there was no sign of any wagons.

Del turned to the mute who pointed northwest. They followed the tracks for a few miles, concluding that the wagons might be hidden in a wash somewhere. They were prepared to search until dark. Determined to find them, Del kept telling himself it was to notify them of the girl's death. But deep down, he wanted to know what kind of people would allow a girl to get caught in a flood.

The mute motioned for him to follow. They cut due west down a dry draw and rode for half an hour. As they rode around the bend four wagons sat in front of them.

▲▲▲

twenty

Delmar and the mute stopped no more than fifty yards from the wagons. Women in sunbonnets sat around a fire nearby. The two men rode forward with caution.

"Hello," Del said, moving closer to the fire.

A woman of about fifty stepped forward. "Can we help you, mister?" she asked in a shaky voice.

"No, ma'am, I came to ask the same. My name is Delmar. I'm the boss of a trail herd headed for Dodge. We mean you folks no harm, but I brought some bad news, I'm sorry to say."

No one spoke.

"Do any of you recognize this?" he pulled the silver cross from his pocket.

One of the women gasped. "Oh, my God." She came forward and Delmar handed her the cross. "It belonged to my Sandy. Do you know where she is?"

"Yes, ma'am, I do. She drowned in the river." He pointed to the mute. "He roped her body out of the river, some miles back. We buried her as proper as we could, ma'am." Del thought the woman was going to faint.

"We're beholden to you, mister. We lost our menfolk some miles back. Indians, you know. Sandy tried to keep us in meat the best she could. We're headed for California. We figured we was too far to turn back. So we planned on keepin' out of sight the best we could and go on."

The mute made a motion with his arm and grinned. Delmar got the message and shook his head. Again the mute pointed toward the herd. Delmar started to curse, but before he could, the mute had dismounted.

The spokeswoman started to say something to him.

"He can't speak, ma'am, but he can hear you."

"Sir, we ain't askin' for no help, but could you tell us if we're in Kansas yet? And are we headed in the right direction?"

The mute was looking over their wagons and livestock. A single team for each wagon, no extra horses. The horses were thin; they needed feed and rest. From what Delmar could see at a glance, they would never make it.

"You're not in Kansas, and you are goin' the wrong direction."

The mute returned and pointed again.

"Okay, okay," Del replied. "You ladies need help. You may not know it, but you do. Your horses won't make it far without feed and a lot of it. The best thing for you to do is to join our drive. We got some extra stock. It'll give yours a much needed rest. Is this all of your company?"

"Yes," the woman said. "There are six of us, that's all."

"Well, ma'am, we got one woman in our drive. Six more won't make no difference. You'll be eatin' a lot of dust, but you'll make it to Dodge City if we do."

The mute motioned for Delmar to go back. He would stay to help them.

Del nodded. "See you ladies in a day or so." He tipped his hat and headed back toward the herd.

As he rode back to the herd alone, Delmar considered his position. He had quit drinking, and he doubted very seriously if he would ever take another drink. It had helped kill the memories at first, but then the whiskey took over. Memories or not, he had to have a drink. Now he was away from it, thank God. That was number one.

Number two, his best friend in all the world, John Roper, had been killed. Who or why had not come to the surface yet. The pin he wore on his hat had not done what he hoped. All three Mexicans except Jingo wore one. Jingo had spoken of it. *Is it some kind of secret organization?* Three times he had been shot at, narrowly missed each time. But since Jingo was killed he had not been shot at once.

Number three, the Thompson men were doing their part with no complaints. Danny Reed, the Thompson foreman, had nothing to say. He and his men just drove cattle. And they did back him up when the outlaws made an attempt to collect.

The herd was moving and he was still alive, but now there were six women coming to join them, and women were trouble, with the possible exception of Nellie. She had never given him a moment's worry. She was accepted as part of the crew.

But he was prepared to accept the women in his usual stoic fashion. He had always met problems head on, the devil take the loser. One thing still puzzled him, though. *Why did Sheriff Bowman insinuate that I killed John Roper? It doesn't make sense.* Del rolled a smoke as he rode. Some day it would all make sense, if he lived that long.

He approached the herd, swung wide of it and headed for camp. It was getting late and he was hungry. As he rode into camp, several men were gathered around Randy Shummer, who lay on the ground. Nellie was putting a bandage on his head.

"What happened?" Del asked as Randy looked up with a grin.

"Not much, boss. Me and Old Slut had a go 'round with a tree. He got mad and I got madder. So the son of a bitch run under a limb and like to tear my ear off."

"Why don't you watch where you're goin'?" Del asked.

"Well, boss, I was. He just don't understand he ain't people."

"Maybe you don't understand he's a dumb steer."

"Hell, boss, he ain't dumb. He follows me everywhere I go. He knows who feeds him corn and salt."

Delmar was satisfied that Randy would not give up Old Slut, but he was about to give up on Randy. He grabbed a plate and left the others to argue it out. He started to tell them about the women, but changed his mind. There would sure be some surprised looks on their faces when the women came rolling in.

The next two days went as smooth as silk. Delmar kept his eyes peeled for the mute and the women. They arrived on the morning of the third day.

Bill Downs rode up at a gallop. "Boss, we got a whole passel of females in camp. And they're clucking around that Mex mute like you wouldn't believe. I never seen the like. By God, I thought ridin' steers was bad enough, but now we're playin' nursemaid. What the hell is gonna happen next?"

Delmar listened until he wound down, then he explained what had happened.

"I'll be damned. The Injuns got their menfolk, you say?"

"Yeah," Del answered. "That's their story, anyway. We can't leave 'em out here goin' the wrong way. Cutthroats or Injuns would find 'em and God knows what would happen. I'll drift on back and check things out."

They had done the right thing, that was for sure. From what Delmar could see they were just a bunch of hidesore grandmas lost on the plains. But a part of him worried about the effect they might have on the men or the herd.

As Del rode into camp, Nellie ran to him. "We got us some company!" she exclaimed as Delmar stepped down from his horse.

"So I see," he said.

The same woman who had spoken for the group before, came forward. "We meet again," she said.

"Yes, ma'am, we sure do."

Nellie looked shocked. "I didn't know you had met."

"Oh yes, Mr. . . ."

"Delmar, ma'am."

"Yes, Mr. Delmar was so kind to offer his guidance and protection. We won't forget this. I know we haven't been properly introduced. They call me Grandma Jones. We want to work, so if there is anything we can do to help out, just let us know. One more thing, we got plenty of food and we're all good cooks."

Delmar smiled. "Well, ma'am, we'll sure let you know when we need your help."

At daylight, the crew lined up for breakfast. The women served, visiting with the drovers to make sure they ate properly. Danny Reed did not like corn bread, but was told to eat it anyway. It was good for him. Each drover was given a heaping spoonful of stewed prunes. Some started to protest, but Grandma Jones insisted. "You haven't had a good meal since you started this drive. I can see that. Your mothers would skin you alive if they knew the way you've been eating."

After the same treatment every morning for three straight days, Randy caught Delmar away from camp and some twenty drovers gathered around. Del knew what was coming.

"Boss," Randy began, "We can't eat the stuff that grandma is puttin' out."

"What's the problem" Delmar asked.

"Damn it, boss, it's them damn stewed prunes. Every drover here has made a shit ring around the camp every morning for a week. Say what you want, but we eat no more prunes."

"Yeah, and that ain't all," Bill Downs added. "My ass is so sore,

I can't set a saddle no more. So we made up our minds, no more of Grandma's cookin'. "

"What the hell did you guys eat 'em for if they gave you the shits?"

"Cause," Randy replied, "she makes you think she's your mother and if you don't eat what she fixes, she raises hell. When I threw mine out yesterday mornin' she seen me. Accordin' to her, I was hell bound, that it was one of God's personal laws that we're supposed to eat everything on our plates. When she got done preachin' to me, I was tempted to pick 'em up and eat 'em dirt and all. I tried to feed 'em to Old Slut, but he wouldn't touch 'em."

"That steer is smarter than you are," Del said. "We don't want the shits. The only thing I can do is to tell Grandma to feed her own crew and we'll take care of ours."

"We don't care what she does, just so long as we don't git no more stewed prunes," Bill said seriously.

Del walked to camp and gathered the grandmas to explain the situation. "No more prunes or else. I can't have all my men down with dysentery."

Grandma Jones agreed, no more prunes, but she would spend her time making fruit goodies for the crew.

"Oh, one more thing," Del added. "If the crew wants to eat 'em, fine, but no more preachin'. "

The next few days went smoothly: no prunes, no dysentery, and no preaching. And Uncle Ted had announced that they were only a week from Dodge. It was an assurance every drover needed. They had all made a thousand plans. Some would drink the town dry while others would probably end up in jail or God knows what else.

Two days out of Dodge City they had unexpected company, Marshall Dillon and two deputies. "We heard you were usin' steers for saddle stock. We didn't believe it, of course," Dillon said with a grin.

"We did it for a while, Marshall. We had to," Delmar replied. "Injuns stole our horses."

"I'll be damned! I never seen anything like it. I could win all the money in Dodge if you'd bring in this herd with the men ridin' steers."

"Like how much?" Randy asked.

"Hell, you name it!" Dillon replied. "This has to be the biggest herd ever to come up the trail. How many you drivin'?"

"Close to seven thousand," Delmar said. "Marshall, if you want, we'll drive 'em right through Dodge on our steers."

"What do you think, gentlemen?" he asked his deputies.

"Well, Marshall, it'd shake Dodge right down to the bedrock. I can see the headlines in the Chicago paper: Herd Arrives in Dodge, Drove in on Steers Broke to Ride, Beef Delivers Beef."

"Okay, Mr. Delmar, bring 'em in. I'll shop around. Might be able to git you top dollar on them steers to boot."

"Like what?"

He looked the herd over. "Well, they're in fair shape. I'd guess twenty-one to twenty-four."

Delmar beamed. "Marshall, we'll drive 'em through fire for that kind of money. You just get set for us, we're comin' in." Delmar and the marshall shook hands and the lawmen rode back toward Dodge.

The word was out, and excitement ran wild among the crew.

"So, we drive the herd through Dodge on our steers. We'll put on a show, by damn!" Randy Shummer swore. "They won't forgit us ever. Me and Old Slut, we'll show 'em."

"Shit," Bill Downs said. "Me and One Way will show you country boys a thing or two when we git there."

Every drover in the crew was bragging about his steer. The names ran all the way from Sweet Mama to Shit Ass. Each was willing to bet on his favorite.

"By God," Bill announced, "we'll put on a Wild West show. We'll race these steers and have us one hell of a good time."

"Not until the herd is sold and loaded into boxcars," Del said firmly.

"You ain't goin' to sell our saddle stock, are you?" Randy asked. "Hell, we can't race our steers if you ship 'em."

No, I ain't sellin' our saddle stock," Delmar said. "I'm givin' every drover one steer as a bonus, so keep your best one."

A whoop went up from the drovers.

"By God, Del, you're my kind of man!" Randy shouted. And the mute smiled and nodded in agreement.

▲▲▲

twenty-one

Delmar put out the word not to push the herd too fast. "Let's give the marshall plenty of time to git organized. We want top dollar for our steers."

There were a lot of sleepless nights in the week that followed. Each drover made plans, grooming his prize steer. Then, on the second day of July, the point rider reported that he could see Dodge City in the distance. Even the grandmas could scarcely contain their excitement as Marshall Dillon arrived.

"By damn, I see you made it," he said with a gleam in his eye. "We're all set, but we weren't sure you'd make it by the Fourth. We generally celebrate a little."

"We'll be there tomorrow," Delmar assured him.

"No, no," Dillon objected. "Hell, one more day won't make that much difference."

"Damn it, Marshall, we'll be dry camped and that'll shrink these steers up. They won't look so good."

"Never mind that! Hell, I think I can get Billingham and Cole to agree to twenty-six a head, providing you ride into Dodge on the Fourth of July on them steers."

Delmar could hardly believe his ears: twenty-six dollars a head. *Them ranchers back home will be rich for a while,* he thought. "Marshall, I'll hold them steers out here for a week for that kind of money!"

"I thought you would. And just for fun, would your boys put on a show for the folks? Like maybe a race? If you will, the city fathers have agreed to put on a big picnic in your honor. The way we see it, the more hell we can raise, the more publicity we'll get back East. That way we'll git more buyers for the cattle and it all kind of works out in the end. Oh, one more thing, we don't mind a little hell-raisin', providin' it's all gentlemanlike."

Delmar agreed to pass the word for his men to have a gentleman's good time. "But I can't promise anything, Marshall. I'll do the best I can."

"I'll be there to help," Dillon assured him, "And I'm pretty good at my job." Dillon waved and rode away toward Dodge.

Delmar sat a full minute gathering his thoughts. A smile spread across his face. It would be one Fourth of July Dodge City would long remember. He was sure of that. The thought of his drovers celebrating in a gentlemanlike manner brought a chuckle. *What the hell kind of celebrating will that be?* But he kept his word, passing Dillon's request on to the drovers.

Randy raised his little finger and said in a high falsetto, "Pray tell us, boss, what is this gentlemanlike hell-raisin'?"

"To be honest, I don't know," Delmar replied.

"Then how in hell are we supposed to do something we don't know how?"

The mute nodded his head in agreement.

Bill Downs turned to him and asked, "Do you know how to raise hell like a gentleman, Mex?"

The mute put his arm around Grandma Jones's waist and began to waltz. The other women whirled around them in a circle, lifting their long dresses just above the ground. The drovers stared in amazement.

"God Almighty!" Danny Reed groaned. "We got to do that by tomorrow?"

The mute did not respond, enjoying every minute of his personal fiesta with the grandmas.

"We got to do that drunk?" Randy asked. "Hell, I couldn't do that on the soberest day of my life."

The mute stopped dancing and joined the crew, sweat streaking his face.

"Is that gentlemanlike hell-raisin'?" Bill Downs asked him. The mute nodded. "Shit, boss, there ain't no way we're goin' to carry on like that for a day and a night. We wouldn't git them steers loaded for a month. It would take us a month to rest up."

"You better grab you a grandma and learn fast, Bill. A gentleman's good time might be real interesting." Delmar chuckled as he walked away.

It was a sight to behold, the grandmas trying to teach ballroom dancing to a bunch of stiff-legged cow riders. The stomping and jumping around went on for half the night with the mute doing his best to help. It was a difficult job, but with no music it was worse.

"If exercise makes your bowels move, the grandmas won't need no prunes for a week," Randy Shummer remarked as he went to his bedroll.

"I sure hope no one seen us," Bill Downs replied. "They'd lock us up for half-wits."

The steers had watched the strange carryings-on for half the night. As Randy made up his bedroll, Old Slut ambled up behind him, giving him a gentle nudge to remind him it was corn and salt time. In all the excitement, Randy had forgotten to feed him. A smile tugged at the corners of Randy's mouth. He went to the supply wagon, scooping up a full quart of corn in his hat. "Here you go, Old Slut. I clean forgot you. I'll bet you think we all took leave of our good sense." As the big beast eagerly ate the corn, Randy rolled up in his bed, some twenty feet away.

It was nearly four in the morning when Randy woke from a dream, so frightened he was afraid to move. In his nightmare, he tried to outrun a stampede when his horse fell, pinning him underneath it so he could hardly breathe. When his sleep-fogged brain cleared, he discovered Old Slut lying almost on top of him. "Damn you, Slut! Git off me." After struggling for ten minutes, he finally succeeded in pulling his blankets and himself out from under the sleeping animal. He stood half-naked in the cool morning air, debating whether to shoot the steer or love him more than he already did.

Bill Downs woke to the sounds of Randy's grunting and cussing. "What the hell you doin'?"

"That damn steer come over and laid down on me," Randy answered.

"Well, don't be so damn tight with your blanket. Give him one."

When daylight came, they found Old Slut lying beside Randy, covered with a blanket. Delmar had to admit he had seen it all. He could accept riding, roping, branding, and chasing steers, but sleeping with one was just too much.

Before Randy joined the crew for breakfast he threatened, "Don't say one damn word to me. It was Bill's idea."

After the laughter died down, Bill drawled, "Hell, I didn't want Old Slut in my bed."

They had just finished breakfast when Marshall Dillon and his two deputies rode up. After a brief greeting all around, they accepted hot coffee, laughing with the crew as Danny told them about Old Slut. "Well, gentlemen, we're all set for you in town. The town council voted all in favor of the celebration."

He walked away from the crew and motioned for Delmar to follow. Out of the hearing of the drovers, he said, "I got good and bad news for you, Delmar. First, the buyers agreed on a flat twenty-five a head. I tried for more, but no dice. And the bad news. I got a telegraph warrant for your arrest. They want you back in Texas for killin' a John Roper."

Delmar's expression did not change.

"Did you gun this Roper feller?" Dillon asked.

"No, he was stabbed in the back in his sleep. Bill found him next mornin' in the supply wagon."

"Do you carry a knife?" Dillon asked.

"No, I don't even own one."

"You got any idea who done it?"

"Yes, I do, but he's dead. When the Indians stole our horses, we found him scalped the next mornin'. "

"I see," Dillon commented. "Is there anything else you want to say?"

"Yeah, if you got the time to listen."

"It's your party," Dillon answered.

Delmar rolled a smoke and slowly began, telling Dillon the whole story. "Every man over there," Delmar pointed toward the waiting crew, "will tell you the same thing."

Marshall Dillon reached over, taking tobacco and papers from Delmar's shirt pocket and thoughtfully rolled himself a smoke. He paused and then said, "You know, that's the damnedest story I ever heard, but I believe you." Dillon lit his cigarette and threw the match away. "What you aim to do about this, the killin', I mean?"

"After the herd is sold, I aim to go back to Texas and somehow prove I didn't kill John, and then, God only knows."

"Well, Mr. Delmar, I'll tell you what I'm goin' to do. As far as I'm concerned, I never seen you. That is, if you give me your word you'll go back to Crooked Fork like you said."

"All right, Marshall, you got it. One more thing, Marshall, I'd like you to be with me when I send their money back to Texas."

"I'll be there, you just say when." They shook hands. "Now git this show on the road," Dillon said.

Dillon and his deputies mounted up. "We'll see you and your cow riders in the mornin'. " He nodded to the crew and rode toward Dodge.

Delmar was deep in thought when Nellie touched his arm. Startled, he turned quickly, nearly drawing his gun.

"Sorry, Del, I didn't mean to spook you."

Delmar grinned. "I was somewhere else."

"Everything all right?" she asked.

"Yeah, sure. We made it; how could anything be wrong?"

"You and that marshall wasn't talkin' about a party."

"You're right. We was talkin' about John's murder and what we was goin' to do about it. We both agreed there was nothin' we could do here. The answer lays somewhere between here and Texas."

Nellie nodded. "I agree. When this so-called shindig is over, we'll talk some more." She patted his shoulder. "You're one hell of a man, Del."

He watched her as she walked toward the chuckwagon, wondering which one of them was more sanctimonious.

▲▲▲

twenty-two

After two dry days, the steers did not care that it was the Fourth of July. As they moved toward Dodge, the only thing on the dumb beasts' minds was water.

Greeted by enthusiastic crowds, the leaders started down the main street of Dodge City at 10:35. The cow riders were putting on quite a show, dashing up and down the flanks of the herd on their saddle steers. Everything was going according to plan until the leaders of the herd smelled water. With nothing in front of them, they began to run. Then all hell broke loose. The screaming crowd, barking dogs, and men shooting in the air added to the confusion as seven thousand cattle stampeded through the heart of Dodge City. As each animal tried to outrun the other, cattle filled the street, running up on the boardwalks, literally ripping lean-to porches from the buildings. Hitching rails, sign posts, and anything in the way came down. A dusty yellow haze hung over the town, so thick that no one could see six feet ahead. The drovers were riding for their lives. Women screamed, men cursed, and the dogs never shut up.

The big white post in front of the bank swayed back and forth a few times before it finally came down with a crash. A half-dozen wild-eyed steers were pushed through the broken windows. Feet and horns flying, they slid every which way on the polished floor, looking for all the world like wild ducks trying to land on a frozen pond.

The leaders tried to stop at the creek for a drink and were pushed on across. Then the herd split, rushing up and down the creek, tearing down fences, trampling yards and gardens. Two hours later they were settled down near the water.

Randy Shummer and Bill Downs sat on their worn-out steers, looking back at Dodge. They were covered with yellow dust from head to toe. Bill Downs started to speak, but instead began to laugh. Randy Shummer glared at him in disgust.

Finally, Bill took a deep breath and said, "I wonder if the marshall would call that a gentlemanlike good time?"

Both Randy and Bill broke into uncontrollable laughter. Bill laughed until tears rolled down his dusty face and Randy nearly fell off Old Slut. Delmar and the other drovers joined in, laughing until their sides ached.

When they had regained their composure, Delmar looked around at the crew. Everyone was present except the Mexican mute. "Anyone see the mute?" he asked.

The smiles left the faces of the crew.

"God Almighty," Danny Reed moaned. "You don't suppose he..."

"Well, let's don't stand here wonderin', " Bill answered. "Let's go find him."

Within minutes the crew had spread out, searching the ground back toward Dodge.

Marshall Dillon straightened his shoulders with a jerk as he saw the approaching riders. The way they were spread out could mean only one thing. They intended to cause somebody trouble and it looked like he was the one. His two deputies joined him.

"God, Marshall," the one on his left lamented, "we can't fight a whole trail crew."

Dillon nodded. "We got to do something to make peace with 'em or they'll finish takin' this town apart and us with it."

Delmar rode in toward Dillon who stood, legs apart, eyeing him. Delmar stopped his horse some ten yards from the marshall.

"Gentlemen," Dillon said, "I know I'm to blame for the stampede, and I don't blame you for bein' mad. I'd be mad as hell myself, but I'm askin' you to use your heads. I know you can outgun us, but think of the good people of this town."

Delmar and his crew sat silent, wondering if the marshall had taken leave of his senses.

"Have you seen a Mexican who can't talk?" Delmar asked.

"Yes, he's with a wagonload of women over at the courthouse," Dillon answered.

"Is he alive?" Delmar asked in the same even tone of voice.

"Yes, sir, he's alive and well. He was shook up some, but he's okay."

Delmar nodded.

The marshall continued. "You got a half-dozen steers in the bank, some more in the Long Branch Saloon, and two or three in the Mercantile. And if you'll change your mind about takin' the town apart, everything is on the house for you and your crew, that includes the girls down across the tracks."

"No more gentlemen's good time?" Delmar asked.

"Like I said, just don't kill anybody."

Delmar turned to his crew. They were still in shock. They were sure they faced a jail term of at least a month. Now things had turned plumb around. The marshall was taking the blame for half tearing the town down, and was making a peace offering to boot.

Delmar wanted to laugh, but he did not dare. He said, "All right, Marshall, but we came to town for a picnic."

The marshall grinned. "Well, let's go make the arrangements." Delmar dismounted and shook the marshall's hand.

Dillon said, "I'll buy the first drink. The town will buy the rest."

Marshall Dillon smoothed things over with the town council. The council agreed that the picnic should continue as scheduled, with steer races the following day.

Danny Reed went looking for the grandmas and the mute. He was told that the wagon had turned over, spilling grandmas all over the street, but no one was seriously hurt. The mute and his steer had been crowded through the window at the Long Branch. He had several small cuts, but the grandmas patched him up. The mute asked Danny in sign language where to find Delmar.

"Having a drink with the marshall," Danny replied.

Delmar finished his drink. "Marshall, we need a bath and a barber."

"Come with me, gentlemen."

As they crossed the street, Delmar noticed several businessmen sweeping up the debris in front of their shops. He, his crew, and the marshall were met at the hotel desk by a small, bright-eyed man who handed them a quill pen. "Sign here, please," he said in a high, squeaky voice.

"Calm down, Dode, this is the Roper crew. They want a bath and a barber. See to their needs and send the bill to the city."

Delmar signed his name and turned to Dillon. "Marshall, we sure thank you."

"Don't," Dillon held up his hands. "I'll see you later when your crew gits cleaned up. The picnic is behind the courthouse."

Nellie and Uncle Ted sat next to Grandma Jones at the first of a long row of tables piled high with food. At four o'clock, Delmar and the crew arrived. They were seated as guests of honor. The local ladies' club waited on them as if they were royalty, bringing each one a tall glass of lemonade, iced to perfection.

As he finished his third piece of chicken, Bill Downs chuckled. "Gee Klist, boss, this is okay. I wonder what that Chink would say if he could see all this?"

Dodge City's mayor, carrying a flag, led a small brass band to the podium. As everyone braced themselves for a long speech, the mayor wiped the perspiration from his brow with a snow-white handkerchief and began. "Ladies and gentlemen, we are gathered here to honor these brave and courageous men. These men are living proof that anything can be done if you try hard enough. They withstood Indians, storms, and even the amputation of this man's leg." The crippled Mexican came forward on a pair of makeshift crutches. "So without further ado, I present the keys to our glorious city to Mr. Delmar."

When the applause and shouts of praise subsided, Delmar stood and nodded to the crowd. As he did, the band began to play. Marching away to the cadence of the bass drum, they left the Roper crew speechless.

For once, Randy Shummer had nothing to say, and the crew spent the hour and a half that followed shaking hands and tipping their hats to the ladies. A pretty Mexican girl winked at Randy and whispered as she passed, "Come to my place tonight, señor." Randy smiled and nodded.

After the crowd had left, Bill Downs sidled up to Randy and said under his breath, "I heard that deal you made with that little señorita. Do you think she has a sister?"

Without turning his head, Randy replied, "Come along and find out."

Delmar motioned for the crew to gather round. "Damn it, men, I hate to say anything, but the people here have really gone out of their way to put this feed on for us. You have to admit they've treated us Texas boys right. So what do you say to..."

"We know what you're tryin' to say, boss," one of the drovers replied. "You want us to tow the line, and I, for one, agree."

The others murmured their agreement, and Randy Shummer winked at Bill Downs.

"Tomorrow at noon, we meet at the herd," Delmar continued. "And thanks."

The drovers took off in different directions. As evening shadows fell, Delmar crossed the street to the hotel hitching rail. He mounted his horse and rode out to check on the herd.

The cattle were doing just fine, grazing on the fresh grass along the creek, occupying some two and a half miles of the creek bottom. Crossing the creek, Delmar rode a half mile up the far side. He had a lot on his mind. He pulled his horse to a halt in a thick cottonwood grove. He dismounted, tied his horse to the low limb of a tree, and walked a short way to a beaver pond. He sat down on a half-rotted log, unconsciously reaching for his tobacco paper. He slowly rolled a smoke, inhaled deeply and put the match out with his boot heel.

"Damn!" he said aloud. He had gotten this far, and although he had his suspicions, he still had not found John Roper's murderer. There was a warrant for him back in Texas, John Roper's estate would have to be settled, and someone would have to run Roper's ranch. There were so many loose ends.

He heard a twig snap behind him. He tensed every muscle, ready to draw, and turned.

"Want some company?" Nellie asked.

Delmar relaxed. "What you doin' out here?"

"I seen you ride out, so I followed you. If you'd rather be alone, I'll ride back."

"Have a seat." He motioned toward the log. "What's on your mind?"

Nellie sat down. "I'm not sure if this is the time or place to tell you. It's something I've been thinkin' about for quite some time."

Delmar slid to the ground, using the log as a back rest. "Good a place as any," he said softly.

Nellie put one hand on his shoulder, turning his face toward her with the other. When he looked up she kissed him long and hard.

"Now you know," she said in a hoarse whisper.

"Do you know what you're sayin'?" he asked.

"Yes, I've tried to tell myself it was crazy, that I was dumb, and God only knows what else. I even got brave and told Uncle Ted. He just looked at me and smiled. When I asked him how I was goin' to tell you, he said 'With your mouth, how else?' I asked him what if you didn't want me. Then what? He said the same thing, 'He's got a mouth, too, you know.' "

Delmar did not say a word. If he was surprised he showed no sign. "Nellie, you know I can't marry you," he began. "There's a murder warrant for me back home for killin' Roper. I didn't do it, but I can't prove who did. John Roper was my first cousin, and as far as I know, I'm his only livin' relative. Both our families was killed in that damn stupid war...."

Nellie put her hand over his mouth. "You think I don't know all this?"

Delmar turned toward her. "How could you know?"

"John told me. You see, Del, John was the one who loaned me the money so I could stay on the ranch. Now I got the ranch and money to operate."

"I'll be damned!" Del said.

"So don't think I came here just to pass the time of day. I know almost everything there is to know about you."

Delmar pulled her toward him. The evening shadows had slipped away and night fell around them. Somewhere below them, a beaver slapped his broad tail on the water. Starlight filtered through the trees, and they lay as one, naked and unashamed.

"How about dinner?" Nellie whispered.

"Yeah," Del replied. "Now you know everything about me."

Nellie nibbled his ear, then kissed it.

Del kissed one of her round, firm breasts again, then rising, he said, "Let's go."

Del pulled on his pants, and Nellie, contented, stretched out on the grass. As she looked up at the moon, words she had read somewhere went through her mind. *The rivers might run dry, the wind might blow, rain may come and drown us all. I'll swear my love for you to all the heavens. "I love you," will be my last words before I die.* Everything else in her life seemed so far away, like a fading dream.

Dodge City was running wide open. Loud music from the bars spilled out into the street. For a moment, they could hear a woman's laughter above the noise. The hotel cafe was still open. Inside, they found a table in a dimly lit corner. As far as Del and Nellie were concerned, no one else existed. No one paid any attention to them and that was the way they wanted it. They finished their meal, then lingered over an extra cup of coffee.

"What's your room number?" Nellie asked.

"Number twelve."

"Mine is just across the hall, number eleven."

"Not tonight, it ain't," Del replied with a gleam in his eyes. He paid the waiter and they walked toward the stairs, hand in hand.

▲▲▲

twenty-three

Randy Shummer and Bill Downs rode their steers across the tracks. "We'll take a look," Randy said. "Then we'll get rid of these steers."

"And then?" Bill asked.

"Who the hell cares!"

They stopped at a half dozen bars, having a drink in each one. Each time, Randy looked around for the cute little Mexican who had so politely invited him, and each time, they moved on to the next with the steers plodding along behind.

Old Slut nudged Randy every once in a while, to remind him it was feeding time. Bill's steer, One Way, not to be ignored, kept a close watch on both of them, making sure he got his share of corn.

In the July heat, the doors to the crowded saloons and dance halls stood open. And as Randy peered into one smoke-filled saloon, he found what he was looking for.

She met them at the bar. "I see you come," she said softly. "Come sit down." She escorted them to a table in the rear. "My name is Eloisa and if you excuse me, I'll be right back." She disappeared into the crowd.

"Damn! She sure is somethin', ain't she?" Randy asked.

Bill sipped his whiskey and rolled a cigarette. "Yeah, she looks better after every drink."

Eloisa returned with a tall girl whose shining black hair hung nearly to her waist. Bill caught his breath. Her eyes sparkled as she smiled with beautiful even teeth.

"This is Señor Randy and Señor Bill." Bill stood, holding his hat in his hand. "Please, Señor Bill, sit down. This is my cousin Rita. Would you gentlemen like another drink?"

"Yeah," Randy replied. "Bring a whole bottle."

A piano and a banjo were playing a lively dance tune. "Come on, señorita. Let's dance," Randy said, and off they went. They danced and drank until they could barely stand.

Halfheartedly, Randy suggested they leave. "After all, we got work to do tomorrow."

But the women prevailed, and Bill and Randy stumbled up the stairs with a half bottle of whiskey apiece and two of the best-looking women in Dodge.

After waiting several hours outside the saloon door, Slut and One Way saw their masters climbing the stairs. Deciding it was feeding time again, Slut led the way inside. Someone in the crowd started yelling, soon others joined in, trying to drag the big saddle steers outside. The more they shouted, the more determined Slut became. He and One Way slowly climbed the stairs, more frightened with every step they took. The stairs shook under their feet, and looking down on the crowd made it worse. To escape the noise, they hurried down the long hall at the top of the stairs. As they went, Slut nosed his way into partly open doors, walking into a room at the end of the hall. With difficulty, they turned around and slowly began to make their way back.

Meanwhile, Randy went out the back door and down the stairs to the outhouse. Without knowing it, he had just missed the steers, which were, at that moment, the furthest things from his mind.

The steers turned around again, spooked by the noise of the crowd below. As they did, Randy hurried through the back door toward his room. The minute he saw his master, Slut lost all fear, while One Way was satisfied as long as he had company. Randy saw nothing in the dark hallway and went straight to his room leaving the door lightly ajar. He pulled off his pants and climbed back into bed.

Old Slut and One Way stopped at the door and waited. After half an hour, Slut gently butted his head against the door. The door swung open and they entered, with One Way following Slut's lead. Standing at the head of the bed, Slut lowered his massive head and sniffed. Well, he got a whiff of the sweetest stuff he had ever smelled. Anything that smelled that sweet must be good to eat, so with his big rough tongue he had himself a taste. It was the back of Eloisa's neck. Screaming, she reached out, touching Slut's cold wet nose. Randy jumped out of bed, groping desperately for his pants and gun belt in the darkness. Trying to back up, Old Slut pushed One Way into the dresser, knocking the bowl and pitcher to the floor. Panicked, One Way swung his great horns to one side, shattering the dresser mirror.

Randy found his pants, held to the floor by a ponderous hoof. Confused, he continued the search for his gun, crawling across the bed on his stomach. Seeing the sudden movement in the darkness, Eloisa drew back both feet and sent Randy flying. He landed on his head at the foot of the bed, jumped up, and ran square into One Way's lowered head. As One Way raised his head, Randy went end over end, landing flat on his back in the hall.

Bill Downs opened his door across the hall just in time to see Randy sprawled in the hallway, naked as the day he was born. Bill grabbed him by the hair of his head and dragged him into his room. "What the hell is going on over there?" Bill demanded.

"I think we got company," Randy replied, rubbing his head.

"Who?" Bill asked.

"Remember, we left Old Slut and One Way outside?"

"Oh, shit." Bill groaned. "You mean they're up here?"

"Yeah, they're in my room," Randy said.

Bill slipped on his pants and lit the lamp. Suddenly realizing he was naked, Randy grabbed a blanket off the bed. Startled, an equally naked Rita struggled to get the blanket back. But Randy refused to give it up, and Rita, seeing a huge bovine head in the doorway, quickly rolled onto the floor and crawled under the bed.

Hearing the commotion, the crowd in the saloon came running up the stairs. The steers, seeking some peace and quiet, decided to go back the way they had come. As they met the crowd at the top of the stairs, the animals took a sharp right turn, finding themselves trapped between a railing and the wall. Wild-eyed with fear, they struggled against the railing until the second floor gave way over the bar.

The drunken crowd rushed back down the stairs to find the cattle belly-deep in broken lumber and bottles. Seeing a mere four-foot bar standing between himself and freedom, Old Slut jumped, sending a table and chairs to splinters on his way. One Way was right behind him.

Caught in the crowd, Randy and Bill, in various stages of undress, were literally pushed down the stairs. A shotgun boomed and the crowd went quiet.

"Git out, all of you!" The bartender stood on top of the bar holding a smoking gun. "Git out, every damn one of you. This place is closed!"

Bill and Randy started to protest, demanding their clothes. But when the shotgun barrel came to rest on Randy's chest, he changed his mind and went out the door hoping to find the steers. Barefoot, he and Bill hobbled along the dark side of the street toward the livery stable, where, to their surprise, they found Old Slut and One Way.

Bill Downs started to laugh.

"What the hell is so funny?" Randy demanded.

"Gee Klist, boss, that's the only whorehouse in history with a real bull in it."

▲▲▲

twenty-four

Delmar woke up with a start. Someone was banging on his door. He tried to call out, but Nellie's arm lay across his throat. The pounding continued. He pushed Nellie away and slumped on the edge of the bed.

"What the hell do you want?"

"This is Marshall Dillon, and I think you'd better come down to the courthouse right away."

"Okay, Marshall," Del yelled back.

"What's goin' on?" Nellie murmured, forgetting where she was. Both of her breasts were exposed above the covers.

Del turned to look at her. "Mighty pretty, little mama."

Nellie started to cover herself, then changed her mind and pulled him to her. She kissed him softly, allowing her breast to brush his face.

It took all of his willpower not to change his mind about the marshall.

"Just so you won't forget," Nellie said. "Now git out of here before that marshall beats the door down."

Del's eyes opened wide when he saw the clock on the wall of the hotel lobby, 10:25. It was almost time to meet the crew.

Whiskey, Guns & Cows

A crowd had gathered in front of the courthouse. Marshall Dillon was at the center, surrounded by a half-dozen Mexicans, all trying to talk at once. As Delmar approached, Dillon drew his gun and fired into the air.

"Damn it! Shut up now. Hear me. Here comes the boss. Talk to him."

The crowd made way for Delmar.

"What's the trouble?" Del asked.

"I am Señorita Eloisa. This is my sister and my cousins. Your *vaqueros* came to my place last night and dees bull you call Slut and another one fell through my place and now I can no open." She paused. "Shit, señor."

Delmar looked at the marshall. "What the hell is she talkin' about?"

"Well, I went down there and took a look. It seems two of your boys rode their steers down across the tracks to have some fun. Well, according to what I've been told, the steers went lookin' for your boys. They wound up upstairs and fell through the floor right over the bar. Lucky no one was hurt."

"Where are my so-called boys?"

Dillon replied. "They're still asleep in the livery stable. One of 'em is wearin' a blanket, the other just has his pants."

"How much damage?" Delmar asked.

"They want five hundred, but I told them two hundred would cover it."

"I'll give em' two-fifty."

"We'll take it," Eloisa quickly replied. "But señor, please don't let them come to my place no more."

Delmar agreed.

Dillon fell in beside Delmar, and together they went to the livery stable. The old man saw them coming and pointed upstairs. They climbed the ladder to the hayloft where they found Randy curled up in his blanket with Bill asleep close by.

"Well, well," Delmar said, shaking his head. Both men opened their eyes. "You boys put on quite a party, I hear."

Randy sat up holding his blanket. Bill sat up holding his head.

"What the hell you two been up to anyway? You got every Mex in town ready to cut you from one end to the other."

"It ain't like you think, boss. We never got in no trouble. There was no fightin' and no shootin', just them damn steers. They tore things all to hell. I promise, boss, I'll shoot that brindle s.o.b.. He has laid on me, bucked me off, and now he's got me thrown out of a Mexican whorehouse."

"No, don't shoot him, Randy. You got a race to win today." In all the excitement, they had forgotten about the races.

"By God, Delmar, you're right. I clean forgot about our speedy steers of chance."

"How about it, Bill?" Delmar asked.

"Oh, my God, it'll take two of those bastards to carry my head."

As Dillon and Delmar started to leave, Randy asked, with great concern in his voice, "Oh, one more thing. Will you git us some clothes? I've been in this blanket so long, I feel like a Cheyenne squaw."

"I'll have those Mexican whores bring your clothes and guns," Dillon said as he disappeared down the ladder.

"I think we're in one hell of a mess," Bill said. "We'll never, never live this down."

The cattle were not forgotten by any means. Delmar made sure they were well-fed and had plenty of water. They could put on as much as a pound a day. He reasoned that one more day before they were brought into the shipping pens, counted, and loaded could not hurt them. Besides, he had never seen a steer race before.

Marshall Dillon had made arrangements for the races at four

o'clock. He wanted pictures, of course, for the eastern papers. At about three o'clock, a crowd began to gather on the street where debris from the stampede had just been removed.

The one-legged Mexican sat in the shade, talking to the mute. The grandmas were gathered around their wagon at the edge of town where the race was to start and end. They had informed Delmar of their plans to remain in Dodge. Manuel the mute had kept his distance from Delmar since they arrived in Dodge. But if Delmar had looked around, he would have seen the mute behind him even when he was rolling in the grass with Nellie. Manuel was aware that Delmar needed time to conduct his business, but he was not about to let anyone harm his boss.

Even after the nightmare of the evening before, Eloisa and Rita were excited about the race. After all, as their cousin said, they had been very close to the bulls, and in the light of day, it seemed almost funny.

Betting was going on all over town. The two deputy marshalls, Hays and Garrison, held the stakes. By the time the race was to start, they had more than four thousand dollars in their possession. Even the banker's wife had secretly wagered a ten spot on Bill Downs's steer, One Way. Old Slut was the favorite after the town found out that he and One Way had torn up the Mexican whorehouse. The Long Branch put up a free dinner for two for the winner, and several other businesses offered prizes.

"Ladies and gentlemen, we are proud to announce that we have twenty-one entries in our first annual saddle steer race. So, gentlemen, mount up. The race is half a mile, one-quarter mile down and one-quarter mile back with no stops. You must cross the line at the far end, turn and come back. The first to arrive here wins. Prizes will be awarded at the Long Branch shortly after the race."

Bill and Randy waited near the starting line. The mute and his big black steer ambled toward them.

"Where the hell did he git that one?" Bill asked.

"He's been trainin' 'im for some time, now," Randy replied.

Tension was running high. One old white-whiskered man shouted, "I'll bet a flat hundred on that steer." Someone covered him immediately.

"Hold your betting, gentlemen."

The steers lined up. The starter fired a gun in the air and the race was on. Spurs, quirts, and cuss words did their work as the competitors left the crowd in a cloud of dust.

Number seven, Sweet Mama took the lead only to be passed by number twelve, Dizzy. The spectators jumped up and down, yelling for their favorites. There was no doubt about it; it was the most exciting thing to ever hit Dodge City.

Even Marshall Dillon shouted at the top of his lungs, "Come on Slut! Come on!"

Nellie and Delmar stood in disbelief. Neither had realized the steers could run so fast. Soon they had turned and were heading for the finish line. Somewhere in the turn, one steer had lost its rider but was still running with the rest. Leaving a dust cloud twenty feet high behind them, the animals thundered toward the finish line. The crowd went into total hysteria. Old Slut was among the leaders with One Way right alongside. The riders were spurring and whipping for all they were worth. The mute's big black steer pulled past Sidewinder. A few yards from the finish line, seven steers ran almost neck and neck.

Grandma Jones forgot herself and shouted, "Slut, you son of a bitch, run!" Another grandma wet her pants. One man got so excited he swallowed his tobacco.

Just as Old Slut broke free from the pack, the big black steer pulled out from the left, and they hit the finish line together.

The crowd quieted down as the judges announced a tie, with a drover named Bell placing third. Randy had lost his hat, and he and the other riders were covered with dust from head to toe. The only distinguishing features were their eyes.

"They wanted a race, by God, and that was the best I ever seen!" Dillon exclaimed. "Them steers are worth a fortune back East."

It was up to the deputies to divide up the money. "We'll pay off in an hour. You winners come and collect."

The Roper crew was lined up at the Long Branch bar. They had seen good times before, but never anything like this: free drinks, free food, and free beds. But they realized it would all soon be over. To everyone's surprise the judges came to find the mute and Randy. Deputy Garrison announced that the winners would divide six hundred dollars, three hundred apiece. The crowd clapped, yelled, and slapped them on the back.

"We're the best damn trail crew that ever came outa Texas!" Danny Reed declared.

"And we got the best trail boss in the whole damn world!" another yelled.

Bill Downs tapped Randy on the shoulder. "Let's git out of here."

When they were alone outside, Randy asked, "What's up?"

"I just thought we might go down to that Mexican place again."

"Oh, God, no, Bill. They made it plain they didn't want us to come back ever."

"Wrong," Bill said. "I talked to Rita at the races. They'll come to our hotel rooms tonight."

"The hell, you say!"

"Oh, yes, my *amigo*."

"I'll go git our rooms; you go tell 'em where to come," Randy suggested.

"You got a deal."

Bill returned within the hour with Rita and Eloisa. He brought them up the back way and the night faded away in pleasure.

▲▲▲

twenty-five

Daylight came early. Bill woke up refreshed, but Rita was still sleeping soundly. He knocked softly on Randy's door and whispered, "Ready to go?"

"Yeah, I'll be right with you," Randy answered, reaching for his clothes as he rolled out of bed. On his way out, he looked down at Eloisa's clothes lying on a chair and a smile spread across his face. He gathered up the clothes, stepped quietly out, and closed the door.

Seeing Randy's idea, Bill went back to his room and returned with a bundle under his arm. They joined the rest of the sick-looking crew for breakfast.

The men worked with king-sized hangovers in the hot sun, pushing the cattle toward the loading pens. They were all corralled by dark.

Late that evening, as Bill and Randy headed toward their rooms to wash up, Bill suddenly stopped at the top of the stairs. "I don't trust those two women," he said.

"I don't either," Randy agreed. "What do you say to changing rooms with Reed and Miller?"

"How we goin' to do that?" Bill demanded.

"Well, I don't know. I just don't want to be in that room tonight."

Randy stood firm. "Let's git a room somewhere else."

Bill was quick to agree and they left the Dodge House and found another room two blocks away.

Delmar and Nellie were nestled together for the third night in Del's room in the Dodge House. At two in the morning, Del woke to sounds of coughing and gagging.

"God," someone groaned, "I can't take no more of this."

Del and Nellie suddenly found themselves coughing and gagging. Holding his nose, Del shouted, "I'll kill whoever put that skunk in this hotel!"

Hotel guests raced downstairs as fast as they could, pursued by the smell of not one, but two skunks. Everyone waited in the lobby until daylight while the hotel management chased skunks and tried to kill the smell. At breakfast, the groggy crew was joined by a wide-eyed Bill and Randy. When they were told what had happened, they did not crack a smile until they were well away from the others.

The cattle buyers were on hand early. Cattle cars had come in during the night, and the long, hard job of loading and counting began. It took three full days before the last steer was loaded.

Dillon and Delmar went to the bank where the drafts for the cattle were issued. Delmar gave directions to the bank for wiring each amount and took equal amounts, according to the number of head, to pay the crew. He paid the $250 to the town for the Mexican whorehouse and prepared to leave Dodge.

"What about your saddle steers?" Dillon asked.

"They belong to the crew," Delmar said.

"Would they sell them?" Dillon asked.

"You can ask them."

He and the marshall found the crew at the Long Branch. It took some talking, but the marshall and the crew finally came to an agreement for two hundred a head. The marshall also agreed to buy several saddle horses.

"I'll be leavin' tomorrow," Delmar told his crew. "I'm goin' to take the train as far as I can, and then the stage. You all got just one week to show up in Crooked Fork. If you don't, I'll figure you're not comin'."

Anxious to get home, over half the crew bought train tickets. After saying good-bye to the grandmas and the rest of the town, they pulled out of Dodge at 10:35, heading east to Wichita, then south to Tulsa.

While Nellie sat beside him, Delmar looked around the crowded car and grinned. There were some ten to fifteen drovers in the car. Uncle Ted, Randy Shummer, Bill Downs, Miller, Boyd, and Danny Reed were sitting proud as peacocks. And in the back corner sat Manuel the mute with his one-legged friend Pancho. Delmar felt good inside. With a crew like this, a man could drive a herd through hell and butcher each one for the devil himself.

It was a long roundabout trip to Crooked Fork. It took three stagecoaches to carry the crew the last five hundred miles. No one in Crooked Fork knew when they would arrive, but Sheriff Will Bowman kept a close watch on the stage line.

He cut the end on a fine cheroot and watched the dust moving toward Crooked Fork. The stage was late, he observed as he opened his gold pocket watch. Will Bowman had made up his mind: the town would sing a different tune when he personally hung Dry Bottle Delmar.

"Damn stinkin' murderer," Bowman muttered to himself.

Ned Thompson assured him that Delmar should hang. The banker, Clem Paterson, was equally sure that Delmar had murdered John Roper. And Will Bowman was sure if Delmar hung, his reelection was in the bag. These and many other thoughts went through Will Bowman's mind as he watched the dust cloud move closer and closer. He checked his gun and glanced across the street, giving the signal to his deputy to be ready. Dry Bottle Delmar would shortly find himself in jail if Bowman had his way.

Swinging wide, the stage turned the corner and set the brakes. It came to a stop some fifty feet beyond where it generally stopped, blocking the view from his deputy. *Damn stupid driver will hear about this,* Bowman thought.

Will Bowman stepped off the boardwalk and crossed the street. Delmar was the third man out, reaching up to help Nellie out. He stepped up on the walk with Nellie on his arm.

"Delmar," Will Bowman spoke loudly enough to be heard by everyone present. Bowman stood with his gun in his hand.

Hearing his name, Delmar turned, pushing Nellie aside.

Sure of himself, Sheriff Bowman said, "You're under arrest, Delmar. I'll take your gun."

The second stage arrived, pulling ahead of the first, but Sheriff Bowman never took his eyes off Delmar. "I don't want to kill you, Delmar. Like I said, hand over your gun."

Delmar moved slowly, deliberately, lifting his gun and holding it butt first at arm's length. "Come and git it," he said, his voice like ice. No one made a sound. Sweat was running down Bowman's face, but he got the courage from somewhere to step forward. He took only two steps and froze in his tracks, facing six men with drawn guns, one a Mexican.

"Don't try it, Sheriff. You might hit Delmar but you'll be dead the minute you pull the trigger," Randy Shummer said coldly.

Bowman stepped back cautiously. *Where the hell was his deputy?* Bowman dropped his gun in its holster.

Delmar did the same, with a thin smile. Then he stepped forward and slapped Bowman's face. "If you ever pull another gun on me, use it! Is that clear?"

Bowman stood with a trickle of blood running down his chin,

his hate-filled eyes afire, like a mad dog. "I will, Delmar, I will," he replied.

Delmar shook with rage. "One more thing. If you want to try me in a court of law, send me a notice. I'll appear. But don't you ever try to put me in that flea trap you call a jail. And you can tell the rest of the narrow-minded bastards in this town the same thing. I never killed John Roper. Now get out of my sight before I kill you."

The crew and the townspeople who gathered around them watched in amazement. Dry Bottle Delmar had made it plain that anyone who wanted to talk to him had better talk without a gun, or all hell would break loose.

In the week that followed secret meetings were held all over the county: in ranch houses, the sheriff's office, at the bank, and among the townspeople. It was nearly a fifty-fifty split, both for and against Delmar.

Delmar took over the Roper ranch, with a good crew and plenty of money to operate. At his insistence, Nellie and her sister Teresa moved into the ranch house.

"What will people say?" Nellie asked.

"I frankly don't give a damn. We said forever, didn't we?"

"Yes, but wouldn't you rather be married?"

"Of course, but there is the possibility I might hang. There's no guarantee I won't. Besides, I want you with me, not twenty miles away."

Nellie smiled. "I know, dear, I know. Uncle Ted and three of my crew can look after things for a while, until something breaks, good or bad."

So with his home life settled, he had a ranch to run.

Just two weeks to the day after they returned to Crooked Fork, a man from town delivered a summons for Delmar to appear in court the eighteenth day of August to stand trial for the murder of John Roper.

Judge Jackson was laid up with a broken leg, and a judge no one had heard of, Judge D. D. Owens, would preside.

Bill Downs asked, "You goin' in?"

"Yes, I am," Delmar replied.

"We'll see that you git there and back," Randy Shummer said.

The mute nodded his head as Randy spoke. He had given Delmar his savings to hold after paying for his one-legged friend's trip home to Mexico. There was no question about the mute's loyalty. Since they returned from the drive, he had tried several times to talk to Delmar, drawing pictures in the dirt. Delmar had tried to understand, but to no avail.

While Delmar waited for the trial, he checked on the taxes on the ranch and money owed to the bank. Surprisingly it was only one thousand dollars. After that was paid, the ranch would be free and clear, with close to twenty thousand in the bank. But the banker was one man Delmar did not trust.

Teresa Stoneman had stayed home while her sister Nellie went on the trail drive. Now Nellie was living with Delmar, a hero to some and a murderer to others. If she loved him, what difference did it make? But Teresa knew the town would talk and Nellie would never be accepted in social circles again. She hoped that Del would be found innocent, if only for Nellie's sake.

Teresa's teaching career had ended when her husband died. After she went to live with Nellie, all the hurt and disappointment seemed like a bad dream. Since they moved to the Roper ranch there was always something to do. But at night she sat alone, watching the lights go out in the bunkhouse. She could hear the laughter, and sometimes found herself blushing at the man talk she overheard.

One evening, Randy Shummer walked up to the main house, tipping his hat to Teresa as she sat in the porch swing. "Is Delmar in?" he asked.

"I'm sure he is. I'll get him." She walked into the house, finding

Delmar in his office. Not realizing Randy had followed her, she turned quickly and he caught her in his arms to keep her from falling.

"I'm sorry. I'm to blame, ma'am. I should of stayed outside." He released her just as Delmar came to the door of his office. He called Randy in and shut the door.

Teresa went back to the porch swing. A few minutes later, Randy reappeared, standing hat in hand in the doorway. "I want to apologize for bein' so dumb, ma'am."

"It was nothing, Mr...?"

"Shummer, ma'am, Randy Shummer."

"Oh, yes, I've heard Del and Nellie speak of you. I'm Nellie's sister Teresa."

"My pleasure, ma'am. Nellie has spoken of you, too," he added. "She said you was a school teacher."

Shyly, she looked down, replying quietly. "Yes, I was. I taught for several years."

Unsure of himself, Randy could not see her eyes and he said haltingly, "It's been a pleasure, ma'am. I guess I better be goin'. Have to be up early tomorrow, y' know. Good night, ma'am." Awkwardly, he backed off the porch and down the steps.

Teresa stood up and took a step toward him. "Good night, Mr. Shummer." She could still feel his strong arms around her. A ghost of a smile played around the corners of her mouth. He was polite and well-mannered, too. She went back to the swing feeling a little foolish.

The breakfast bell clanged and the men walked from the bunkhouse to the cook shack. Delmar had just stepped off the porch to join them when one of his men shouted a warning. A half dozen heavily armed Mexicans with guns drawn rode around the corner of the hay barn. It was plain they meant business.

Delmar quickly stepped back on the porch and ran to where his gun hung on a peg in his office. He slipped out the back way and stood directly behind the Mexicans as they held the crew at gunpoint. The six spoke Spanish among themselves and then one asked the crew a question in Spanish, but no one answered. He tried again, but still no answer.

Their clothes were ragged and dirty. They all wore large sombreros, spurs, and had tall-horned saddles. From what Delmar could see at a glance, they were Mexican outlaws. Three stepped down from their horses to collect the men's guns.

"Hold it right where you are or you die." They did not understand English, but they understood that someone behind them would shoot. The tone of the voice told them that. They stood perfectly still with their hands in the air. "Git their guns, men," Delmar ordered.

One Mexican nervously turned toward his horse, and Del shot his sombrero off. Then he said harshly, "I said don't move."

Within a few minutes, they were disarmed and lined up on the ground.

Hesitantly, Nellie and Teresa stepped out onto the porch. "What are they doing here?" Nellie asked.

"I don't know," Del said. "I don't speak Spanish."

"I do," Teresa spoke up.

"Well, ask them."

She spoke with the tallest one for a few moments and told Del, "He wants to talk to Mr. Roper."

"Tell him Mr. Roper is dead. What does he want with Roper?"

According to the Mexican, Roper was supposed to send money back with Jingo. When Jingo failed to return, they came to collect the five thousand dollars they had been promised.

The mute was late for breakfast, but as soon as he saw the Mexicans, he drew his gun, making signs that he would shoot them.

Delmar shook his head. Excited, the mute tried every way he could think of to tell Delmar who they were. Finally, he made a sign that he wanted to write, and Teresa brought him paper and pencil. Teresa read as he wrote.

He pointed to the pins in their hats. He said they were outlaws, and that Jingo was part of their gang. They had once fought the president and lost the same as John Roper, and they were going to fight the blue soldiers from Mexico. John Roper had given them money once and they wanted more.

"Please, patron," he wrote, "shoot them and Mexico will thank you."

"Randy, Bill, you men guard the Mexicans. Take them inside. I got me an idea. Teresa, you're a godsend."

Nellie hugged her sister. "You just might have cleared Del."

After the crew had eaten their breakfast and fed their prisoners, Delmar called Bill Downs into the house.

"If you're goin' to do what I think you are, God help us," Bill said.

"What makes you say that?" Del asked.

"Cause Sheriff Bowman and Ned Thompson have sworn to kill you on sight. Ben Thompson won't have anything to do with Ned, says he's crazy. The Thompson brothers are splitting up, each taking half of the ranch."

"When did you hear this?" Del asked.

"Danny Reed told us yesterday. He made a special trip to tell us. He quit the Thompson brothers and asked me for a job. I told him I'd have to ask you. Ben Thompson told the sheriff if he wanted to go on living he'd better back off and leave you alone. But for some reason, the banker is out for your scalp and he's holding something over the sheriff. So now you know. What do you want me to do?"

Delmar stood, rubbing his whiskered jaw. "I didn't think they were that bad," he admitted. "I thought Ned would forgit all his wild threats after I sent them their money for the herd."

"Remember, boss, I'm the one who shot Ned Thompson."

"You think my memory's that short?" Del snapped. "But I was

the one who told him to git off his ass and move his cattle. I heard him cussin' as I rode away. He swore he'd kill me. I just hope he doesn't hire a crew to back him up and come to town huntin' trouble."

"I don't know about Ned Thompson bringin' in a bunch of gunslingers. But Danny was for damn sure tellin' the truth."

"I'm sure he was," Del said. "There's only one place to hold these Mexicans, and that's the jail in town. With the mute writin', Teresa readin', and these guys as proof of what he says, it'll clear me."

Bill exploded. "Bowman won't lock these guys up! Hell, he'll turn them over to Ned Thompson. That'll just add fuel to the fire."

"Bowman may not lock them up, but I will." Delmar glanced at Nellie who stood by with a worried look on her face.

"That means only one thing to me, boss. We'll have to take over the jail. And that means nothin' but trouble."

"Maybe so," Del agreed. "But I have only a few days before the trial. Whatever I do, it better be right."

Bill nodded. "Well, we can't stand here jawin' all day. Let's take 'em to town and see what Sheriff Bowman has to say."

Del pulled his hat down, confirming his decision. "Let's saddle up."

▲▲▲

twenty-six

Bud Lackman of the Crooked Fork Mercantile saw the Roper crew and their prisoners coming down the street. "Lord God and all that's holy!" he said to his wife as she joined him at the window. "There'll be blood runnin' in the streets. I just feel it in my bones."

"I told you that a long time ago," she snapped. "Delmar's nobody to make fun of."

"Right as usual," he muttered under his breath.

Sheriff Will Bowman crossed the street, headed toward the oncoming riders. As he stood in front of his office across the street from the courthouse, a cold feeling came over him. His stomach churned and the stub of a cheroot hung loose in his mouth as he squinted into the sun. Just seeing Delmar could mean only one thing: trouble. He had to make his word good. He had sworn to everyone in town that Delmar would hang for the murder of John Roper. But so far he was still running loose, and Bowman had not mustered the courage to shoot it out with him. The town refused to come to his aid—even his deputy was home in bed asleep.

Delmar drew rein at the hitching post right in front of him. "Hello,

Whiskey, Guns & Cows

Sheriff," he said coldly, "I brought you some prisoners."

Bowman looked shocked. This was not what he had expected. "What did they do?" Bowman stammered.

"Let's just say they were trespassin' for now." Del dismounted. "I want to hold 'em 'til Judge Owens gits here."

"In my jail?" Bowman asked.

"Yes, in your jail."

"Hell, they ain't nothin' but a ragtag bunch of Mexicans. You ain't goin' to hold them here. Bedsides, I can't take your word on this. You're wanted for murder. Why don't you just run their asses back to Mexico yourself?"

"Sheriff, I'm goin' to tell you just once more. I want them locked up."

Bowman had a feeling that these Mexicans had something to do with John Roper's murder. Somehow Delmar wanted to use them against him. "No, I won't. Handle it yourself, and remember, you're the one that's wanted."

Delmar drew his gun so quick, Bowman did not even see it until it was pointing at him. "Now git inside or I'll break your skull." Del walked forward, pushing Bowman ahead of him with the gun barrel.

The crew did not need to be told what to do. Dismounting, they led the Mexican prisoners inside.

As he left the hotel, Danny Reed noticed the horses in front of the sheriff's office and crossed the street to investigate. He had planned to talk to Delmar about a job. Seeing the brand on the horses, he realized he would not have to make the ride. The mill iron R stood out like a sore thumb, on the left hip of each animal.

Bill Downs met Danny at the door and stepped outside. Danny could hear Bowman raising hell inside.

Danny smiled. "What happened to him? Did Delmar step on his tail?"

Bill said, "Yeah, Del asked the sheriff to hold some Mexicans 'til his trial. Bowman wouldn't do it, so Del persuaded him."

"Hell, He'll let 'em out soon as Del leaves."

"No, I don't think so. We're not leavin' town 'til Judge Owens gits here."

Danny Reed got the picture real quick. Delmar and the Roper crew were taking over the jail and Sheriff Bowman could do whatever he was big enough to do.

"How are you and Ned Thompson gettin' along?" Bill asked.

"Just the same since he and Ben split up. Ned has been hirin' every stray man he can find. Ned and the sheriff are thicker than two warmed-over biscuits. Ned claims Del shorted him on the herd money, and Bowman said he would add robbery to the warrant."

"You know better than that," Bill said. "You and Marshall Dillon was right there in the bank when the drafts were made out."

"I tried to tell 'em that," Danny went on, "but I might as well have been talkin' to one of those steers we drove. Bowman thinks if he can hang Delmar, he'll win the election. Ned wants him dead for his own reasons. Ben Thompson is doin' all right. Most of the crew went with him when they made the split. He promised the foreman's job to Art Tucker because he was older and had more experience than me. Ben made him ranch boss while I was on the trail drive. But Ned claims he ain't nothin' but a broken-down saddle bum."

"That sounds like Ned." As Bill spoke, Delmar and the sheriff came back out of the door.

Bowman was still telling Delmar how high he would hang. Losing his patience, Del grabbed him by the collar and said, "If I hang, you'll be the deadest sheriff in or around Crooked Fork. Now shut up before I put you out of your stupid misery." He pushed Bowman away from him. "Somebody give him his gun."

As Randy Shummer handed it to him, Bowman backed into his office, shouting, "Don't show up here again 'til Judge Owens comes to town. Now git the hell away from here."

Whiskey, Guns & Cows

Delmar gathered his crew around him. "Men, I want to tell you how it is. As you can see, I just took the law into my own hands, and I may have to do it again until I get a fair trial. God knows Bowman will run to Ned Thompson and others will join up with 'em. So if you want to go back to the ranch, just go. I don't want to git you all hung. I just hope the judge will listen."

Bill Downs spoke for the whole crew. "We wouldn't miss this for another night in Dodge City. We ain't goin' nowhere. We talked about this last night and everybody here aims to see you through this mess."

Seeing Danny Reed, Del said, "How you been, Danny?"

"Fine," Danny said.

"Heard you was lookin' for a job."

"Yeah, sure am."

"Well, do you want to join this square dance?"

Danny smiled. "Couldn't be any bigger than we went through already. I never did think you killed Roper."

"Do you know who did?" Delmar asked.

"Well, I know one thing; you didn't git shot at anymore after Jingo got killed in that Indian raid."

Del looked surprised. "You noticed that, too. That's the reason I got those Mexicans locked up. They were part of Jingo's bunch."

Danny nodded.

"Well, boss, what do we do now?" Bill asked.

"Go over to the hotel and git set for whatever. We'll leave a couple of men here to guard the jail."

Danny Reed was deep in thought.

Del asked him, "What's on your mind?"

"Well, boss, I wouldn't do that."

Everyone turned to look at him. It was the first time any of the men had disagreed with Delmar.

"Speak up, man." Del encouraged him.

141

"Well, I been thinkin'. If we were all over at the hotel, the sheriff and a bunch of men could come hellin' into town and cut us off from the jail. It seems as though we're goin' to be here a week or so. Why couldn't we bring in a chuckwagon and bed rolls and just set up a camp right here in front of the jail?"

Looking the situation over, Delmar turned to the crew. "Now, that's the best idea I've heard yet. We'll do it."

Bill Downs laughed. *What a hell of a surprise for Will Bowman and his friends. They are about to see the town drunk in action.* Within an hour, the whole town knew that Dry Bottle Delmar had taken over the jail. But even as that news was being circulated, the Roper crew was on the move.

At 4:20 that same afternoon, a chuckwagon and two feed wagons pulled up in front of the jail. On another side of the building, a fire was being built and pots and pans were being set up. A dozen men with bedrolls and horses were setting up camp in the middle of town. No one was sure what was going on, but the townspeople were convinced of one thing: the town drunk intended to stay a while.

The news spread through Crooked Fork and the surrounding countryside like wild fire. Some of the ranchers could not believe their ears. But when Jack Miller heard about it he called a meeting of his men. "Delmar is in trouble, and I aim to help him. I was on that trail drive, as you all know."

His ranch was small compared to most; he had five men. His foreman was a big dark-skinned man from Louisiana. At first, his men had a hard time understanding his Cajun accent, but they got used to it. Everyone called him the Cajun. Jack Miller sent a man named Sandy to tell other small ranchers what was going on. He left two men at the ranch. Jack Miller, the big Cajun, and Sandy would meet in town.

"Somebody mad at the gatherin'?" The Cajun asked, as he put on his gun belt and secured a long thin knife. The *gatherin'* is what he called the town of Crooked Fork.

"Yes, a friend of ours is in trouble, Cajun. I got to go help him."

The big Cajun turned to the men who would stay at the ranch. "I'll see you a while ago. I am at the gatherin' when you see me, if you want to."

Delmar sat beside the fire drinking coffee as Miller and his men rode in. Seeing the camp in the middle of town, Miller chuckled to himself. They joined him at the fire, and Del explained about the Mexican prisoners and why he had finally sent Bowman packing. He was sure he would be back with help.

Miller said, "I've put the word out. There'll be more men coming."

The big Cajun placed tobacco in a cigarette paper and rolled it with one hand, then lit it with a burning stick from the fire. He turned to Delmar. "You not on this jail for dance. The gatherin' not mad, eh?"

Confused, Delmar looked to Miller.

"He asked you if you were serious about holdin' the jail and if people in town were mad at you."

Delmar wanted to smile, but he did not. "Yeah, I'm serious about this jail. I don't know how people feel, but I've been told it's about a fifty-fifty split. So far nobody's said anything to us one way or the other." He pointed over his shoulder at the jail. "It's my only hope to clear myself."

The big Cajun stood up. "I go to the gatherin'. I see you a while ago."

Del understood. The Cajun was going to find out for himself. He did not look like a man who took anybody's word for anything.

"Where did you git him?" Del asked Miller.

"I hired him about three years ago. He came ridin' in one day. I kinda liked him, so I gave him a job. I never been sorry either. He's a good man."

"How the hell do you understand him?"

"Sometimes I don't," Miller admitted. "But we git along."

"He looks like he'd be good with horses," Del went on, "and in a free-for-all, look out."

"That's the reason I brought him along."

Del had posted lookouts on every road into town. He wanted to know the minute Ned Thompson and Sheriff Bowman came to town looking for trouble. He knew they would, but when?

More men rode into town, two and three at a time. Most of them came looking for Delmar. They were either ranchers who had ridden with him or men sent in their place. Within three days, some thirty men were eating and sleeping at Delmar's camp.

The big Cajun kept in touch with Miller, telling him who was for them and who was against them. The attitude of most people was to wait and see what the judge decided.

▲▲▲

twenty-seven

Sheriff Bowman did exactly what Del expected; he went straight to Ned Thompson. When he arrived with the news of Delmar's takeover, Ned was outraged.

"We should go in there and take that two-bit drunk apart. I got just the crew to do it."

"I'm sure you have," Bowman agreed. "But don't you think that's just what he wants you to do?"

Ned stopped pacing the floor. "You're right. We would just get a hell of a lot of men killed. But I got an ace in the hole they don't know about."

Bowman sat on the edge of his chair. "You do?"

"You're damn right I do. I sent for a man that can take care of that damn drunk and anything he can come up with."

"Who?" Bowman asked.

"Lefty Hellman."

Bowman's heart skipped a beat. "He's damn expensive, ain't he?"

"Yeah, he cost me a thousand which you can add to the company expense if he gits Delmar."

"When will he be here?"

Whiskey, Guns & Cows

"Tomorrow," Ned answered. "He's bringin' some of his boys with him."

"Good," Bowman replied. "We'll just leave it up to Hellman to git Delmar, then things'll quiet down. He has done nothin' but cause trouble ever since he came here. I've had him in jail a dozen times. God, I wish I knowed then what I know now. I would've shot him without blinkin' an eye."

Bowman felt better after talking to Ned Thompson. But as he rode toward town, he kept remembering Delmar's draw. Now he had the jail and men to back him. Maybe with Delmar out of the way they would still insist on a new sheriff. Somehow he had to convince them Delmar was wrong and he was right. So far no one was running against him—maybe no one would. Then no matter what happened, he would still be sheriff. But down deep, he knew that was too good to be true.

Bowman arrived in town, keeping his distance from Delmar's camp. Ned Thompson was right. They were waiting for him. Bowman went to the Westside Bar, several blocks away from the hotel. He needed a drink, and he pushed through the swinging doors.

Several men lined the bar. Standing at the far end were three men. One wore a left-handed gun. Their clothes told him they had come from the border. They must be the men Ned Thompson had hired. Making his way toward them, he leaned on the bar and ordered a whiskey. The bartender left the bottle, and Bowman tossed off his first drink in one gulp.

"Can I buy you gentlemen a drink?" he asked.

"Sure," the one closest to him answered. "Never turn down a free drink, even from..." Seeing the star pinned on Bowman's vest, he hesitated. "The law," he said.

"Welcome to Crooked Fork." Bowman held up his glass. The other three did the same and tossed off their drinks.

"We got some more ridin' to do. See ya, Sheriff." The same man spoke for the rest.

They left the bar, mounted up, and rode off. As Sheriff Bowman watched them through the windows, he thought, *Hell will break loose tomorrow and Delmar will be dead.* His thin lips curled in a cruel smile. *Ned Thompson will see to that.*

The stage came and went every day. Delmar and his men watched for any sign of Judge Owens. The trial was only two days away. Several cowboys unknown to anyone came and went, but the routine stayed the same.

That afternoon, they gathered around the lee side of the jail, out of the wind, sipping coffee. The waiting had become more boring by the day. A tall, well-dressed man joined them, carrying a notebook in his hand. Randy Shummer offered him coffee, thinking he was a rider from some nearby outfit, or possibly a news reporter.

"Do you do much writin'?" Randy asked.

"Sometimes," he replied in a slow Georgia drawl. "I heard about this trail drive an' thought I'd get a few facts and make a note or two."

"You could a got all that in Dodge city," Miller said, throwing a stick toward the fire.

"I just come from there. I met a gentleman up there, Marshall Dillon. He strongly suggested I come here. So here I am. I'd like to meet Mr. Delmar."

Hearing his name, Delmar looked up. "That'd be me." Del stood up, helping himself to fresh coffee.

"I know it might be tiresome for you to tell me the whole story from start to finish, but a lot of people would like to know."

"You writin' the story?" Del asked.

"You might say that."

Some of the men grinned. "Don't forgit to tell him about Randy, Bill, and Old Slut," Miller volunteered. The crew laughed.

"No, I won't forgit that," Delmar said. "I bought a Mexican whorehouse," Then he pause, deep in thought. "All right, Mr. . . ."

"Just call me Darrell."

Delmar nodded. "Let's go over to the hotel and I'll tell you the whole story from start to finish. Maybe I can remember a thing or two that will help me when Judge Owens gits here. Sure wish he'd hurry up. This bunch is eatin' a beef a day."

They went to the hotel cafe, ordered pie and coffee, and Delmar sat back and told his story while Darrell made notes.

"One question, sir. Why did you bring this camp to town?"

"Well, for two reasons. First, to keep a close eye on them Mexican prisoners, and second, to make damn sure they're here when the judge shows up."

"I take it you're expectin' trouble from this Ned Thompson you mentioned and the sheriff?"

"Among others," Delmar added.

"What will you do if this Judge Owens doesn't show up?"

"Damned if I know. He'd better show up or this whole damn country will go to war. Like I told you, I ain't guilty, and damned if I'll be pushed around."

"I believe I have enough notes, Mr. Delmar."

"You're welcome to roll your bed in the chuckwagon if you like. Breakfast is at six."

"I'll do that, and I thank you for your hospitality."

When Delmar returned to the campfire, the Cajun was waiting for him. Miller spoke first. "You got big trouble, Del. Ned Thompson hired a fast gun and the talk is he wants to meet you at one o'clock tomorrow right here in town."

"Has this fast gun got a name?" Del asked.

"Yeah." Miller kicked the dirt with his boot toe. "It's Lefty Hellman from down on the border. We can git our men set up and when they show we can take 'em."

"No, Miller, I'll meet him."

"He ain't alone," Miller protested. "He's got two men with him. I ain't no good with a gun, but, by damn, I'll do what I can."

The Cajun smiled at Del. "Some boss," the Cajun said, "You and me, huh?"

"I can't ask you to do my fightin'."

The Cajun grinned. "You and me, we make the war, you'll see."

Again Del looked at Miller. "He said you and him would straighten out the town," Miller translated.

The Cajun finished his coffee and went to his bedroll.

▲▲▲

twenty-eight

Ned Thompson leaned back in his big leather chair. Seated across from him was Lefty Hellman, a man Lefty called Arkansas, and Three Fingers Donlin. Two of Joe Donlin's fingers were missing on his left hand, shot off by an outlaw down in Mexico. Although he was marked for the rest of his life, he had the satisfaction of killing the man who had done it. His gun was for hire to anyone with enough money. Lefty Hellman had found Three Fingers in El Paso and they picked up Arkansas in Big Bend. They waited patiently as Ned Thompson counted out one thousand dollars.

Sheriff Will Bowman watched the transaction. Clem Peterson also watched, sweat trickling down his face. He had personally delivered the money to Ned Thompson.

"Well, gentlemen, there's your money."

Lefty Hellman picked it up.

"I want to warn you," Ned continued, "this damn sure ain't no pushover. Dry Bottle Delmar is smart, and damn good with a gun to boot."

Sheriff Bowman nodded his agreement.

"We'll see about that," Lefty replied. "I sent him word to meet me at one o'clock tomorrow. So if he ain't runnin', we'll be there."

"He won't run," Clem Paterson assured him. "Just how do you intend to do this job, as you call it?"

Lefty grinned, revealing tobacco-blackened front teeth. "Well, from what I've seen, there ain't no way of hidin' an extra gun in one of those buildings. An' if he's as smart as you say, he'll have his own men posted. So the only way is to call his hand. If it's a fair fight, we can't be arrested for murder. If it ain't fair, we won't walk away—his crew'll cut us to pieces. It has to be fair, no other way. I don't much like the idea. I like the upper hand, but in this case it's man against man."

Clem Paterson could not believe his ears, men killing other men for money. But even he had considered committing suicide if the trail drive failed. Now if Delmar was killed, he stood a good chance of coming up with a plan to take over the Roper ranch. There were ways of coming up with a hidden mortgage. His attention was again directed to Lefty as he spoke.

"Just so we understand, gentlemen, one thousand now and two more when the job is done."

Peterson and Bowman looked shocked.

"That's right, gentlemen, the banker here with one and Bowman with one."

"I never agreed to any thousand dollars," Bowman said as he stood up.

"You have now," Lefty said coolly, "You're a witness to this transaction, so you're as guilty as anyone present."

A faint smile crossed Ned Thompson's face; he liked Lefty's style.

Clem Paterson did not like it at all. He knew Bowman did not have one thousand dollars, which meant he would have to loan it to him. It was getting damned expensive, but he was not in a position to say *no*. He began to wish he had kept his mouth shut about Delmar. He should have trusted John Roper's judgment.

The look on Paterson's face told Ned Thompson what he wanted to know. Paterson was a miserable excuse for a human being. Thompson had the upper hand and he intended to use it. "You got a deal, gentlemen. Mr. Paterson will have your money at the bank when the job is done." Thompson took a brown bottle from his desk drawer, set glasses out, and began to pour. "I want to warn you again, gentlemen. Delmar is a bad son-of-a-bitch, and I got a hole in me to prove it."

They tossed off their drinks.

"To tomorrow." Ned stood and held up his glass in a toast.

The ride back to town was a long one for Bowman and Paterson. They had traveled for half an hour before Paterson spoke. "Where you goin' to get your thousand dollars?" he asked Bowman coldly.

"Simple, my good man. You're goin' to loan it to me."

"What makes you think so?"

"If you don't, Lefty and his men will take your bank apart."

"That's just what I thought," Paterson replied. "There's one more thing I want to get straight. I want you to make sure Lefty gets the job done. 'Cause if you don't, I'll up the ante. I'm quite certain Lefty could make sure we have a new sheriff."

Bowman understood very well, and as they rode toward town he considered a plan to make sure Delmar did not walk away. It was his big chance. If everything worked out right, that smart-mouthed banker would have to loan him money whenever he wanted it. For a moment he wondered, *How much would Delmar pay for what he knew? But that won't work. I've pushed Delmar too far.* A cold chill came over Bowman. *What's to stop Delmar from killing me if he lives past tomorrow?*

Paterson rode silently, engrossed in thoughts of his own. He was angry he had allowed himself to be caught in Ned Thompson's web. Just by delivering the money to the ranch, he became a witness to the transaction. Bowman was a witness, too, and was already trying to blackmail him. *Would Bowman ever stop, or for that matter, would Ned Thompson? How could he have been so stupid?* He realized he would be far better off if Delmar lived. It was not Delmar he wanted dead, but Bowman and Ned Thompson.

He cast his eyes toward Bowman. He would never have a better chance. The small pistol he carried inside his pocket suddenly weighed ten pounds. He had never killed a man before, and he trembled at the thought of it. As Bowman rode just ahead of him, Paterson pulled the pistol from his pocket. The cold metal felt good in his sweating hand. How he ever pulled back the hammer, he did not know. As he fired, his horse jumped at the sound, and Sheriff Bowman slumped forward over his horse's neck, desperately trying to hang on. As he fell, the animal shied away from the body.

Spurring his horse into a dead run, Clem Paterson did not look back. He had done it. One witness was dead.

The lights of Crooked Fork came into view. He rode straight to the livery barn with the sheriff's horse trailing behind. The old man who ran the livery was asleep. Paterson thanked God for that. As far as he knew, no one had seen him ride out, and no one was on the street when he returned. He did not bother to unsaddle the horses. They went inside on their own.

Paterson walked to his house. *No one will dare suspect me of murder. Even if they do, how can they prove it?* Safely inside, he picked up a bottle and poured himself three quick drinks. Feeling the comforting fire in his stomach, he sat down and put his feet up.

After Ned Thompson's housekeeper woke him the following morning, he paced the floor like a caged lion. He told himself over and over again, "This has to work!" *But why do I still have doubts?* He had no doubt about Lefty Hellman: killing was his business. *So where do my doubts come from?* He paused, staring at the bottle on the table. He started to pour himself another drink. *Why should I do that?* he asked himself. *I'm gettin' as bad as Dry Bottle. Damn! Why am I so worried?*

As he sat down, he remembered what Bill Downs had told the crowded courtroom before the trail drive. There was no better man with a gun than Delmar. *Well, there would be today.* He would see to that.

The sky was turning pink in the east. Light began to fill the room. Ned Thompson did not bother to blow out the lamp on the table. He took a rifle down from the rack and checked it over, putting a few extra shells in his pocket. He went to the corral, caught a horse, put a saddle on and cinched it tight. He mounted and rode toward town. If he timed it right, he could be there by one o'clock.

He refused to hide like a damn skunk. If Lefty did not get Delmar, he would kill him himself. Nobody would expect a thing like that. A crooked smile crossed Ned's face. It was all very clear to him. He would wait until the shooting stopped. If Delmar was still standing, he would ride out from behind the hotel and personally gun him down.

Deep in thought, he was suddenly brought back to reality when his horse shied to the opposite side of the road. As he quieted the animal, he saw something out of the corner of his eye. Sheriff Will Bowman lay dead in the road, shot in the back.

"I'll be damned," he said aloud. "I never thought Paterson had the guts." Paterson was the only one who could have shot him. Lefty and his men had taken the back road, and no one else had been to the ranch since Paterson and Bowman left. The only tracks were of their horses.

Ned dismounted and rolled a smoke. There was only one reason for Bowman's murder: he was a witness to Clem Paterson's presence at the exchange of money between himself and Lefty Hellman. With Bowman out of the way there was only one witness left. "Me," Ned said aloud. "Just me."

Whiskey, Guns & Cows

Paterson must have figured out the trap Ned had set for him. The dead sheriff was proof of that. Ned had just wanted a little insurance to keep the banker on his side. He looked down at the body. He was not about to put the dead sheriff across his saddle and ride into Crooked Fork. Everyone would know he was in town in a matter of minutes. He had more important things on his mind than a two-bit sheriff. His kind was a dime a dozen; the country was full of Will Bowmans.

As he rode into town, Ned stayed out of sight of Delmar's camp. "Who the hell ever heard of setting up a cow camp in the middle of town?" he asked himself. He checked his pocket watch; it was eleven o'clock. He had a two-hour wait. He put his horse in the hotel livery stable. No one would pay any attention to it there. With no better place to pass the time, he stayed near his horse, out of sight.

The weather had not changed; another hot day was in store for Crooked Fork. The men grumbled, but had no intention of leaving. They had gotten word of the showdown, and each determined to make the best of a bad situation, right or wrong.

Their thoughts were interrupted by the arrival of a surrey. Uncle Ted and Nellie rode in front, with Teresa and the mute in the back seat. Uncle Ted drove the team to the back of the chuck wagon and stepped out, helping the women down. Delmar came forward, casting an angry glance at Uncle Ted. Ted shrugged his shoulders. The trip was not his idea.

Nellie was the last person Del wanted to see. She saw the look in his eyes, but threw back her head and stood her ground. Whether he liked it or not, she had come.

"I don't know what you folks are doin' here, but I want you out of here within the hour."

Nellie shook her head stubbornly. "Not this time, Del. I know there's goin' to be trouble, and I belong here with you. It's my fight, too."

"Not this time, you say?" Del repeated. "I don't want you in danger. Can't you understand that?"

Disgusted, he threw his cigarette away. "Damn it, Nellie, go back to the ranch and let me do my job."

Tears filled Nellie's eyes. She knew what he was trying to tell her, but she wanted to be with him, especially in time of trouble.

Del turned on his heel. "Goddamn it, Ted. Git these women out of here."

Fire in his eyes, Delmar was fighting the old memories of the Kansas border raids. Seeing his wife raped and his two children killed, he swore he would kill Major Hallet and damn his soul to hell. He shot him in the face while the good major begged for his life. Del remembered well what he had told the major before he killed him. "You immoral son of a bitch! You've raped and killed your last woman." Then with pleasure, he pulled the trigger and watched the back of the major's head splatter against the wall of his house.

That afternoon, Delmar had the same cold gut feeling. Sometime that day, he would have to kill again. No one could tell where a stray bullet might go. He had lost one woman to a damn senseless war, and he did not want to lose another. It was shocking to him, but he loved her. All the love he had for his murdered wife seemed so far away.

Manuel the mute came forward. He took Nellie by the arm and pushed her toward the surrey. Nellie pulled away. She threw her arms around Del's neck and kissed him. "I love you," she whispered. She turned and slowly walked to the surrey.

Teresa and Randy Shummer stood nearby. Del heard him say, "You go on now. I'll watch out for him."

"I'm worried about you, too," she replied.

"Don't worry about us. We got an army around here."

Ted drove away with the women, but the mute stayed behind. It made Del feel good, just knowing he was there. Del spoke to him and they walked away from the camp. The Cajun joined them. It was then that Del realized he was going to face a showdown with a Cajun who could hardly speak English, and a Mexican who could not speak at all.

▲▲▲

twenty-nine

Darrell, the tall graying man who had taken notes on Delmar's story, emerged from his bedroll in the chuckwagon that morning. Noticing extra activity, and being naturally curious, he decided to have another talk with Delmar.

"How are you today?" he asked.

"Not so good," Delmar replied as he carefully checked his gun. "I can't be in two places at the same time." He dropped the gun in its holster and continued to flex his hand.

"I don't understand, sir. I thought everything was going well."

"It was until yesterday." The question in the man's eyes kept Delmar talking. "I'm supposed to be in court today at one o'clock, if the judge gits here."

"The judge is here."

Del looked up quickly. "You see him?" he asked.

"Yes, I saw him."

"I sure wish I could," Del went on. "They've brought in some hired guns, and they sent word they would meet me at one o'clock. That makes it a little difficult, don't it?"

"But I'm sure the judge will take that into consideration."

Del nodded. "He might not have anyone to try if I don't beat this fella to the draw." Del almost spoke in a whisper.

"Do you think you can beat him?"

"I don't have any choice. It's him or me."

"Is that expert gunman here in town?"

"Yes, along with half the country. I wish to God people would just let men settle their difference without all the big show."

"I agree with you, Mr. Delmar. However, so-called professional gunmen die all the time because they think they're faster than someone they heard about. It goes on and on and will continue forever. Who are we to stop it?" The big man pulled two cheroots from an inside pocket and offered one to Delmar.

"No, thanks," Del replied.

After he lit it and got it going to his satisfaction, Darrell pulled a watch from his vest pocket and glanced at the time. "You have a half hour, sir."

Del nodded. The camp was unusually quiet. The men had a lot on their minds. *What if?* was the big question. It crossed his mind as Delmar checked his gun for the tenth time.

The big Cajun stood up, rubbing his hands together, as he squinted into the sun. Manuel the mute checked his guns. He spun the cylinders, making a series of clicking sounds.

The rest of the men began to spread out. It was their job to make sure everything was fair, to make sure that no hidden gun shot anyone in the back. The crew had gone over every inch of the town. No one was to remain on a roof or in an upstairs window. It was an unwritten law.

Randy Shummer checked his gun while Bill Downs adjusted his gun belt. The one thing none of them could stop was time. It passed without interference. At straight up one o'clock, Delmar nodded to the big Cajun and Manuel the mute. They stepped slowly out into the main street of Crooked Fork, moving deliberately toward the Crooked Fork

Bar at the far end.

Uncle Ted and the women had not obeyed Delmar's orders. Nellie insisted on being as close to Del as possible, and the closest place Ted could think of was the jail. After all, Delmar was camped in front of it. Pulling the surrey to a stop, he tethered the team and they walked unnoticed into the jail.

Nellie could not force herself to go home. She had to see for herself. She could not sit idly by, waiting to hear his fate from someone else. God had taken one man away. Would he be so cruel as to take another? "Del is all I'll ever ask of God," she whispered as she watched him walk, flanked by Manuel the mute on his left and the big Cajun on his right.

She blinked back the tears, her heart pounding inside her chest. She caught her breath as she saw three men coming from the bar. With catlike grace, they moved as one down the center of the street toward Del and his men. She suddenly realized it would be only a matter of minutes before they met. She felt a scream form in her throat, but nothing came out.

Teresa and Uncle Ted stood transfixed at another window. They could just as well have been made of stone. There was no wind; nothing moved except the men on the street. Nellie felt her knees weaken, and her ears began to roar. As the darkness engulfed her, her hand slipped from the window. Suddenly she was falling, and there was no way she could stop. She kept falling, falling. Far away, she heard the sound of gunfire, like a distant clap of thunder. She heard Teresa say, "Oh, my God!" She heard footsteps and another gunshot, then all was quiet.

She found herself in the sheriff's swivel chair, with Teresa and Uncle Ted putting cold rags on her face. Slowly, the room stopped spinning.

"Is he. . . .?"

As he walked, Delmar tried to understand why the men at his side were there. They could be marching straight into the jaws of hell. He wanted to say something, but it was too late. Neither man hung back, there was not a break in their stride. He had seen the same thing in the war, men willing to die for what they believed in. They were ready to sacrifice themselves, to end their lives. Some did it for money, like the men he was about to face. Others did it for love, loyalty, and a dozen other reasons. But the reason above all was so that they could call themselves men.

As Delmar stopped, the big Cajun moved over some six feet and Manuel the mute did the same.

Lefty Hellman stopped some fifty feet away, his arms folded across his chest. "Hello, Cajun, long time no see. I never thought I'd see you on that side of the line."

"Good gatherin', good man," the Cajun replied.

Lefty nodded to Delmar and the mute, confident, almost cocky. "No hard feelings, it's just another job."

Del wanted to tell the gunman that pay dirt might come pretty high, but he held his tongue.

Lefty said, "Shall we proceed, gentlemen?" He slowly lowered his arms to his sides, his left hand only inches from his gun.

Delmar did not look at his men. A shift of the eyes could get him killed. His one thought was for Lefty Hellman, to wait, to watch for the slightest sign that he was going for his gun. Delmar could not help but remember the time he faced Crazy Bill Anderson. It was the same, except that it was just he and Crazy Bill. Del saw the muscles ripple under Lefty's shirtsleeve. Delmar's gun was in his hand and his first shot was on its way before he realized it. His reflex was faster than his mind would accept. His first shot was dead center just as Lefty's gun cleared leather and came up in line. Del's second shot was simultaneous with Lefty's first, but Lefty's had pulled off center. Del felt the slug tear through him, and the last thing he saw was Lefty going down. Still clinging to consciousness as he hit the ground, Del struggled to get up.

Manuel the mute drew both guns. Two slugs spun Three Fingers around, but not before he pulled the trigger of his own gun. The mute felt his leg give way as he fell toward Delmar. Only the big Cajun was still standing, wiping the blood from his jaw where a bullet had broken the skin. Delmar was still trying to get up, and the big Cajun helped him.

"Too slow, too slow," the Cajun said, pointing to the three on the ground in front of them. "We make good war, eh?"

Delmar tried to smile. The big Cajun spun his gun around his trigger finger and dropped it back in the holster. Suddenly, Del saw a horseman coming straight at him. With his last bit of strength, he pushed the Cajun aside and drew his gun. He recognized the rider; it was Ned Thompson with a rifle at his shoulder. He was coming at a dead run.

Rifle fire cracked behind Delmar, and Ned Thompson's rifle flew over his head as he tumbled out of the saddle. His horse stopped as it had been trained, waiting for a command that would never come.

Suddenly, the street was filled with people. Delmar felt himself surrounded, then he saw Nellie. As she took hold of his arm, everything started to go 'round and 'round, then everything was gone.

Bill Downs stood in the shade of the hotel overhang. Why he had his rifle, he had no idea. It just seemed right for someone to have one. He watched the gun fight. It was a fair one, but then he saw the horseman come from out of nowhere. Once before, he had seen this same man lift a rifle to his shoulder. With the rider in his sights, Bill squeezed the trigger and watched Ned fall. "This time I didn't miss," he said dryly as he stepped down off the boardwalk.

Manuel the mute struggled to his feet, but managed to stand only with Randy Shummer and Jack Miller's help. They took him to the hotel where a doctor examined his leg. The bullet had gone through just below the hip. There were no broken bones, and the doctor quickly dressed the wound.

As they carried Delmar in, the doctor shooed the crowd away and closed the door. The bullet would have to come out. From what he could tell, it had just missed the right lung. After half an hour of probing and sweating, he had the bullet out. "Here," he said to Nellie. "This is a souvenir." Her hand shook as she accepted. "He'll be all right," he assured her, "but he'd best spend a long time in bed."

"Can we move him?" Uncle Ted asked.

"Yes, I think so. I'll give him something to help him sleep, understood?"

Nellie nodded.

The Roper crew loaded up their wounded.

The doctor told Nellie, "I'll be out in a day or so."

▲▲▲

thirty

When Delmar opened his eyes he found himself home in bed with Nellie sitting beside him. As he tried to move, pain shot through his chest.

"Could I have a drink?" he asked weakly.

Nellie's eyes snapped open. "I'm sorry, I must have dozed off. Welcome back," she said softly, reaching down to brush the hair off his forehead.

When she returned, the big Cajun was with her. He held Delmar's head while he drank. Even swallowing was painful, but Delmar did not complain.

In a matter of minutes the room was filled with people. Teresa and Randy Shummer stood to one side, holding hands. Del did not need to be shot again to tell what was happening there.

"We're goin' to git married real soon," Randy stammered. "We wanted you to be the first to know."

"Well, I'm real pleased." Delmar winked at Randy.

After the others had left the room, Nellie sat on the edge of the bed.

"I got to git to town and see that judge," Delmar said.

"No, you don't. The judge is here. He came out with the doctor."

"How long have I been here?" Del asked.

"Two days," Nellie replied.

"I never heard of anybody sleepin' two days."

"The doctor seen to it that you did."

"I suppose they got me hung by now," Del said slowly.

"No, I don't think so. I'll get the judge."

A tall, gray-haired man entered the room, the same man who had taken all the notes on Del's story.

"Where's the judge?" Del asked.

"I'm Judge Owens."

"I'll be damned. I'll just be damned."

"I should have told you right away, but sometimes a judge likes to get things firsthand. A lot has happened since the shootout. Ned Thompson talked a lot before he died. He swore that the banker, Mr. Paterson, shot your local sheriff. He also admitted that he hired the men to kill you. His last words were, 'Damn that drunk's soul to hell.' I got the feeling he didn't like you."

"What about me?" Del asked.

"You're in the clear, with the help of Manuel, the one you call the mute, and Teresa. There's no doubt that Jingo killed John Roper. The Mexicans you put in jail are all wanted in Mexico, I understand. I'll see that they're taken back to the border. That leaves only one question."

Del could only guess.

"Who would you recommend for sheriff? I need someone I can work with."

"There is one man I would recommend," Del said. "Danny Reed. If I were you, Judge, I'd ask Bill Downs about it."

Bill Downs walked into the room. "Pretty easy life you're livin'," he said.

Del smiled faintly. "Not bad, but I'll trade you."

"No thanks, I'll pass."

"Bill, this is Judge Owens."

"We've met."

"He wants to ask you a question."

"He's been askin' me questions for two days," Bill answered. "One more won't hurt."

"What do you think of a Mr. Reed for your local sheriff?"

Bill looked at Delmar. "That's what he wanted to know?"

Delmar nodded his head.

"Danny would make a good one," was Bill's reply.

Judge Owens excused himself. "I'll see you before I leave."

As Nellie came back into the room, Bill stopped at the door and turned to Delmar. "Gee Klist, boss, that was some fight." Holding his sides in pain, Delmar began to chuckle.

Nellie's face lit up. She could not remember when she had heard Del laugh. If that was what it took to make him happy, she would learn to speak Chinese. Her first attempt was, "Gee Klist, boss, I love you. Hurry up and get well. There should be two of us in that bed."

▲▲▲

If you enjoyed this
book, please write to
James Lawrence
Box 272, Newport, WA 99156